$3.95

Down the Hatch

JOHN WINTON

DOWN THE HATCH, John Winton's new novel about the redoubtable Lieutenant Commander Robert Bollinger Badger, alias The Artful Bodger, and the strange goings on in the Royal Navy catapults his moonstruck crew aboard a submarine. Afloat or ashore, under the Bodger's benevolent command, the *Seahorse's* submarine company gives proof positive that there are more things in the British Navy than the men in Whitehall dreamt of in their rather limited philosophy.

Despite Admiralty qualms, both Bodger and *Seahorse* emerge triumphant. They wave the flag with such success at Oozemouth that they are greeted at every subsequent port of call by a new batch of letters on delicately tinted and perfumed writing paper from the grateful city's enraptured females. Exercise "Lucky Alphonse" is a resounding victory for The Bodger. *Seahorse* "disables" U.S.S. *Little Richard*, the largest warship the world has ever seen, and returns from the "battle" unscathed, despite the relentless pursuit of Black Sebastian, otherwise Captain Jasper Abercrombie Sebastian Persimmons, D.S.O. and bar, D.S.C. and bar, the greatest submarine hater in the Navy. The episode of the amorous whale is humiliating, but never reaches the ears of Whitehall while

(Continued on back flap)

DATE DUE

SEP 1 3 1983			
JAN 7 1984			
JUN 1 9 1984			
OCT 1 9 1985			
MAR - 2 1986			
DEC - 2 1990			
MAR 1 1 1992			
AUG 1 1 2000			
GAYLORD		PRINTED IN U.S.A.	

Down the Hatch

Down the Hatch

JOHN WINTON, pseud

ST MARTIN'S PRESS

Salvador Dali tells a fable of a sardine
on the seabed who, seeing a submarine
pass overhead, says to his children:
'There goes our revenge: a great tin
made of sheet-iron in which men, covered
in oil, are held inside, pressed against
one another.'

1

The pictures on the walls of the Admiral's private office were all mementoes of a long career in submarines. By the door there was a group photograph of his submarine training class: three rows of grinning sub-lieutenants and a bearded training officer. Next to it was the Admiral's first command coming to a buoy in Portsmouth Harbour; her elementary wireless aerials and angular conning tower had not been seen at sea for many years. More submarines followed, a string of them, growing longer and sleeker through the years. The last picture of the sequence was the barrel-sided submarine depot-ship which had been the Admiral's last sea-going command. The other pictures were a mixed collection: a periscope photograph of a broken-backed Italian cruiser sinking against a pale Mediterranean sunset; a fox-terrier wearing a sailor's cap; and a startling picture of a submarine returning from her last patrol, flying the Jolly Roger, with her ballast tanks ripped in great gashes where a Japanese destroyer's screws had raked her.

The Admiral was not a sentimental man but he had held on to his pictures. They had travelled the world with him, survived all his removals and, he hoped, would go with him into retirement.

The Admiral himself was something of a celebrity in the Submarine Service. He had married very young and to the envy of his contemporaries, capturing by far the best-looking of the Admirals' daughters to come out between the wars. He had had a stormy career, so stormy that many of his friends regarded it as a miracle that he had ever achieved the rank of Rear-Admiral; his enemies attributed it to a triumph of matter over mind. He had trampled roughshod over his opponents. He had never toned down his scorn for superiors he thought incompetent. Tact and finesse were unknown to him; he had achieved everything by brute driving force. His tactlessness had led him to one court martial, two D.S.O.s, and three lung-splitting cheers from every ship's company he had ever commanded. He was of the school who learned about men rather than machines and who put charity before technique. But now the old fires were damped. The Admiral was left with a row of medal ribbons and his pictures. He often thought of retiring from the Navy and sitting for an agricultural constituency in the West of England.

The Admiral's favourite view was from his office window (he had coveted the view since he was a sub-lieutenant). From where he was standing he looked out over the submarines where they lay at their trots. The nearest submarine was charging her batteries; a plume of spray and steam rose from her after-casing and the Admiral could hear the thumping of her main engines against his window. Ahead of her another submarine was loading torpedoes. The Admiral could see the dull blue shape of a torpedo being lowered into her hull.

The furthest submarine was the longest and largest of all. She overlapped her neighbours at both ends. Her tall fin soared above the stubby towers of the rest. She was painted dead black except for the white identification numbers on her fin and she was plainly brand new. The Admiral looked at her like a father recognising his favourite daughter.

The Admiral allowed himself to gloat over her for a minute and then, as though struck by a painful memory, scowled and turned away from the window. The Captain who was standing on the other side of the desk braced himself apprehensively.

Captain S/M was the Admiral's opposite in temperament. He was what was known in the service as 'a charmer.' He was in command of the submarine squadron which operated from the base and he was well used to the Admiral's moods. He had often been the sounding board for the Admiral's hobby-horses. But it was not often that he was so peremptorily summoned into the presence. Captain S/M guessed that the Admiral must have something pretty serious on his mind.

'Sometimes,' the Admiral began, sadly, 'I really wonder why we bother. We've all fought for years to get the Navy a new submarine instead of a new block of offices. We've fought, and beaten, every government department. We've fought every branch of the Navy. We've fought everybody from the Ministry of Pensions to the Y.M.C.A. to get this damned submarine. At last we got her approved. We got her designed, we got her started and now, by God, we've even got her finished. In spite of sympathy strikes, wildcat strikes, token strikes and every other bloody kind of strike. At last we got H.M.S. *Seahorse*, God bless her and all who sail in her. Admittedly she's obsolete. She was obsolete before she was even designed. That's not the point. The point is that we've survived the worst the trade unions can do, we've survived two changes of government, three changes of First Lord and four financial crises to get her.

9

And now that she's finished her work-up and is ready to join the fleet, what happens? We find we can't choose a captain for her. The whole thing is taken out of our hands. We get some passed-over bumpkin nobody's ever heard of . . .'

'Oh, not exactly, sir,' Captain S/M put in tactfully. 'He was my Torpedo Officer in my first command.'

'Has he ever commanded a submarine himself?'

'He had an old V-boat just after the war, sir.'

'Exactly! An old *V-boat*! *Seahorse* is not an old V-boat! She's the best submarine we've got now and the best we're likely to have for a damn long time! What's this man been doing all these years?'

'I gather he was training cadets for a while, sir. Then he had a job in the Admiralty and one in Bath. And he was Jimmy of a cruiser in the Far East for a commission, sir.'

'Why did he leave submarines?'

Captain S/M blushed. 'I understand it was because he wrote "Quoth the Raven" in the visitors' book after dining with the Admiral, sir.'

The Admiral's manner softened. It was a coup worthy of himself when young.

'Who was the Admiral then?'

'Admiral Creepwood, sir.'

'Ah yes, I know him well. And Flora too, come to that. Her curried shrimps once gave me the worst attack of Malta Dog I've ever had. But that's beside the point. This man may be an excellent trainer and a first-class pen-pusher. He may be an excellent First Lieutenant in a cruiser. He might even be something of a gastronome but why, *why* send him here to command *Seahorse*? I've got a list of submarine captains as long as my arm, any one of whom could take her.'

'Sir, can't you . . .?'

'I've tried, I've tried. But Their Lordships are adamant. But why, that's what I cannot understand?'

'It may have been, sir . . .' Captain S/M hesitated.

'May have been what?'

'It may have been your remarks to the First Lord about new blood in submarines, sir.'

'But I meant the *submarines*, not the officers! Oh my God,' said the Admiral plaintively, '*when* will I learn not to talk to politicians like that? Their minds just don't work like other people's.'

'I think this man will be all right, sir, when he gets back into practice.'

'He'd better,' said the Admiral.

The new Commanding Officer of H.M.S. *Seahorse* was at that moment walking along the jetty towards his submarine. He was a stout, red-faced man with a shock of black hair which was just beginning to go grey. He walked with an unconcerned but hopeful air, as though he expected at any minute to be offered a drink. His name was Lieutenant Commander Robert Bollinger Badger, D.S.C., R.N., but he was known throughout the Navy as The Artful Bodger.

Nobody looking at The Bodger's jaunty step and nonchalantly-pursed lips could have guessed that inwardly The Bodger was as nervous as a frightened kitten. As Captain S/M had told the Admiral, it was several years since The Bodger had commanded a submarine and now, by some ironical twist of circumstance (The Bodger had long ago stopped trying to unravel the mystical processes which decided officers' appointments in the Navy) he had once more been given command of a submarine. Furthermore, his new command was not just any submarine, but the latest, the fastest and the most expensive the Navy possessed.

Looking at *Seahorse*, The Bodger could see that he had been entrusted with a thoroughbred. Her lines rose smoothly from her low tapered stern to her high flared bows. Her sides had none of the gratings and awkward projections of older submarines. Her fin seemed to grow from her body in a clean proportioned sweep. Even The Bodger's predecessor, a venerable submarine captain who had been appointed to stand by *Seahorse* while she was building because he had an unsurpassed way with dock-yard officials, had been moved to remark that she seemed a reasonable design.

The Bodger was pleased to notice that the trot sentry was ready to salute him and was wearing a clean pair of gaiters. As he mounted the narrow gangway, The Bodger felt that, after an unconscionable length of time in the wilderness, he was coming home at last.

The rest of *Seahorse's* officers were waiting in the ward-room. They had all met the new Captain and they were agreed that he seemed a reasonable fellow but they knew that first appearances in submarines often turned out to be wrong. They realised, equally, that their social and professional lives during the coming commission depended to a very large extent upon the Captain's personality. The history of the Submarine Service abounded in stories of the brilliant and kindly men who had commanded sub-marines. But there were also darker tales of evil-tempered or eccentric men who had driven their officers, and par-ticularly their First Lieutenants, over the edge of break-down. The wardroom were well aware that, for them, the new Captain was more powerful than Caesar and more terrible than Jehovah.

The Bodger dexterously flicked his cap so that it slid along the chart-table and wedged itself behind the echo-sounder. Then he parted the wardroom curtains and, while the rest stood up, sat down in 'Father's Chair,' at the end of the table.

Seahorse's wardroom was typical of many in the Submarine Service. A central table was flanked by seats, upholstered in blue plastic material, which could be converted into bunks. The bulkheads were panelled in light polished wood which was broken up in several places to allow passage for pipes and valve handwheels. The spaces between the bunks were fitted with cupboards and drawers and, along the top of one bulkhead, a bookcase. A barometer and a clock were set into the woodwork above Father's Chair and a deep depth-gauge faced them on the opposite bulkhead. The whole space was slightly smaller than the driver's cab of a long-distance locomotive and, at sea, provided the living, eating and sleeping space for six men.

'About time the bar was opened,' The Bodger said.

The wine cupboard was quickly opened and glasses and bottles set out on the table. The wardroom noted the remark; the Captain's policy about the bar was vital.

The Bodger raised his bubbling glass.

'Here's to us. Whores like us.'

'Cheers, sir,' said the rest of the wardroom, cautiously.

'Well now,' said The Bodger. 'I've managed to thrash out most of our programme for this term with the Staff Office. It's not very exciting but it could be much worse. Tomorrow, we're going to sea for exercises by ourselves. This is for my benefit, to give me a chance to get a grip on things again. But if anyone has any ideas about any particular evolution, now's your chance. How about you, Number One? Have you got anything you feel strongly about?'

'Not really, sir, though we might have another go at things like putting out a fire in the battery, sir. We weren't too good at that during the inspection.'

'Good, we'll certainly do that.'

Frederick Wilfred Garnet de Zouche Burnham, the First Lieutenant, once delighted his kindergarten teacher by confiding that he wanted to be an angel when he grew up. The kindergarten teacher, a kindly soul, had thought it a heavenly idea. The family, however, had thought differently. By tradition only the second son joined the Church. Young Wilfred, the third son, was therefore delivered, scarcely protesting, up to Dartmouth at the age of thirteen. He was a shy, fragile child with long fair hair, a thin nose and green eyes. He had quickly acquired the nick-name of Vera, a name which still returned to haunt him whenever members of his term were gathered together. But the boy with the ethereal looks and the frail physique had won a reputation for survival; he had served with three of the toughest and most unpleasant captains in the Navy List and he had never been logged nor goaded into losing his temper. The First Lieutenant of Wilfred's first submarine had been driven into the arms of the psychiatrists by a captain who asked him, every morning at breakfast throughout a two-year commission, whether he felt well. Wilfred had watched and noted and said nothing. The Bodger suspected that his new First Lieutenant had qualities of withdrawal which made him immune to the boorish habits of people whom he considered his inferiors.

'How about you, Chief? All parts taking an even strain in your part of ship?'

'Yes, sir.'

Derek Masonwyck, the Engineer Officer, was the wardroom's senior lieutenant and oldest inhabitant. He had joined *Seahorse* before she was launched, before she had even been a ship and was still several hoops of steel on a wet, windy slipway. He had stood by her while she grew from a shell into a submarine. He had watched and advised while she was transformed from an imaginary conception, represented by lines on thousands of drawings, into a solid entity with life and dimensions. He was a small man, with hunched shoulders as though from much crouching in the basements of submarines. He alone of the wardroom had known The Bodger when he had last been in submarines and while he remembered The Bodger as an excellent fellow, he had yet to be convinced of his qualities as a submarine captain. The Bodger recognised that Derek would probably be the hardest member of the wardroom to win over.

'Well, if nobody has any ideas about tomorrow, we'll leave that and see how we get on on the day. The day after tomorrow we set off for Oozemouth to show the flag. The idea is to show the great British public that we actually have got a submarine that Nelson didn't fly his flag in. . . .'

'Oozemouth?' said Dagwood Jones, the Electrical Officer. 'I had a great-aunt who lived there once.'

Dagwood Jones had a sharp, ferret-like face and black hair brushed straight back on his head. A degree at Cambridge, at the Navy's expense, had left him unusually erudite for a naval officer and he still wore a faintly donnish air, as though he were merely present in *Seahorse's* wardroom to lend a little tone to what would otherwise have been classified as a thieves' kitchen. He had a waspish sense of humour and a disrespectful choice of words which had often run him foul of senior officers.

'She used to breed miniature pekingeses and was a wizard at the horses,' said Dagwood. 'She made a lot of money in half-crown bets. My mother told me the biggest wreath at the funeral was from the local bookie!'

'Have we got charts of Oozemouth and all that, Pilot?'

'Oh yes, sir. Everything's under control in that line.'

Lieutenant Gavin Doyle, R.N., was the ship's Navigating Officer and lady-killer. He had thick curly black hair, blue eyes, full lips and a reputation of which Don Juan himself might have been envious. Gavin's taste for fast sports cars and svelte girl-friends provided gossip for most of the Wrenneries in the Service.

The last member of the wardroom, who had not spoken and who in fact very rarely spoke, was Rusty Morgan, the Torpedo Officer and the ship's sports officer. He was a large, placid officer with red hair and a pleasantly freckled face. He was a particular friend of Dagwood's, being as good-humoured as Dagwood was prickly. He had played rugby football for Dartmouth and for every ship and shore establishment he had served in since and was now on the verge of a Navy trial. The Submarine Service thought of him as a resoundingly good chap and the finest open-side wing forward to join submarines since the war.

'We'll stay six days in Oozemouth,' The Bodger went on, 'and sail immediately for Exercise "Lucky Alphonse." That lasts three weeks. After that we get a fortnight's maintenance here and then go off to the Equator somewhere to do something for the boffins, but that hasn't been settled yet. And that's as far as the Staff Office crystal ball goes. By the way, Number One, I almost forgot to tell you, we've got a Midshipman R.N.V.R. joining us for training. He's a National Serviceman and I understand he's pretty green. I don't know exactly when he's joining . . .'

There was a knock outside and the curtain was flung aside. The Bodger's jaw dropped open.

Framed in the doorway was a very parfait young naval officer. His doe-skin uniform still had its virginal sheen, his patches were dazzlingly white, his buttons blindingly bright, his cap stiffly grommeted, and his face was composed in a grimace of concentration. Just visible behind him was the dazed countenance of the trot sentry.

The apparition gave The Bodger an elbow-cracking salute.

'Midshipman Edward Smythe, R.N.V.R., come aboard to join, sir!'

The Bodger recovered himself.

'Ah. Ah, yes. Do come in.'

'Aye aye, sir!'

The Midshipman seated himself in the one vacant chair and fixed The Bodger with a stare of furious zeal. The Bodger was disconcerted.

'Do take off your cap and hang it somewhere, old chap,' said Wilfred.

'Aye aye, sir!'

The Midshipman whipped off his cap and held it, peak forwards, on his lap. The Bodger winced.

'Slow down a bit, Mid. Relax. What are you going to have?'

'What am I going to have, sir?'

'Yes, what would you like to drink?'

'Oh. Can I have a glass of beer please, sir?'

'Beer?'

'*Beer?*' The wardroom looked at each other as though the Midshipman had asked for a draught of hemlock.

'We don't keep beer,' Derek said mournfully. 'We haven't got room for it.'

'Can I have a glass of sherry, please, then?'

'*Sherry?*'

Dagwood began to search in the wine cupboard.

'Sherry, sherry, sherry. We've got a bottle somewhere. Derek won one in a raffle.'

'Have a horse's neck, Mid,' said The Bodger kindly. 'It's brandy and ginger ale.'

'I'm afraid I've never tried brandy, sir.'

'How old are you, boy?'

'Twenty, sir. Nearly twenty-one.'

'Nearly twenty-one and you've never tried brandy,' said Dagwood.

The wardroom gazed at the Midshipman as though he were an aborigine newly emerged from the remotest depths of the Matto Grosso.

'Anyway, you've come just at the right time, Mid,' said The Bodger. 'Always join a new submarine when the bar's open. Softens the blow a bit. On both sides.'

'I'm sorry I didn't come earlier, sir. I only heard about it as I was going into lunch. I didn't get an appointment or anything. Someone just stopped me and told me.'

Wilfred snorted. 'Good heavens, you never get *appointed* to any submarine. You just think to yourself, I think I'll relieve old Charlie in the good ship *Venus*. So you stand up at the bar inboard and when anyone asks you what your next job is you just say, *I'm* going to relieve old Charlie in the good ship *Venus*. You keep saying that and after a month or two a little man calls you into his office and tells you, in the strictest confidence, that your next job is to relieve old Charlie in the good ship *Venus!*'

'Don't you believe it, Mid,' said Dagwood. 'If you do that you'll find yourself in a boat day-running from the Outer Hebrides with a Quaker wardroom and a Captain S/M whose wife you insulted at the last Summer Ball! No, the answer is to get a monk's habit and walk around the depot-ship, genuflecting every fifteen paces and chanting from S.G.M.s . . .'

'I'm afraid I don't know what S.G.M.s are, sir.'

'S.G.M.s stands for Submarine General Memoranda. Equal to but under the *Koran*. Every night at sunset the duty submarine staff officer climbs up to the roof of the Admiral's office and rings a bell whereupon all submariners all over the world turn and face Gosport while the chapter for the day is read out. My God, you'd better bone up on S.G.M.s, Mid. When a submariner is buried he's laid out like a Crusader with his sword in one hand and his copy of S.G.M.s in the other!'

The Bodger saw the beginnings of panic in the Midshipman's face.

'Now that we're all together for the first time,' he said firmly, 'I want to make a few points about the way I intend to run things in this boat. I don't intend to do this again. I hope this will be the last time I'm going to talk in this rather pompous manner. As you all know, I've just come back to this after rather a long absence. I'm out of practice and I look to you for your full support while I get my eye in again. My way will probably be quite different to the way you did it in your last boats. But different boats, different cap tallies and I expect you to back me up in whatever I'm doing. I shan't hesitate to replace any officer who doesn't. In return, you can be sure that I will back you up all the way. I think that's enough for general matters. Now for particular things. Drinking. Your winebills are no concern of mine unless you choose to make them so. All of you, except the Midshipman, are sufficiently experienced to know when enough is enough. When I first joined submarines we weren't allowed to drink down in the boat while we were alongside the depot-ship. We had to do all our drinking up in the depot-ship where Commander S/M could keep an eye on us. I'm not suggesting any such arrangement nor do I intend to set an arbitrary limit on how much or what you drink but you can be sure that I'll come down like a ton of bricks on any officer I find drunk on duty. Now, smoking while dived. Various captains have various ideas on this. I'm going to try a new way and abolish the old "One All Round" idea altogether. I'm going to allow smoking anywhere in the submarine while dived except in the control room, where there will be no smoking at all unless the submarine is on the surface. I don't know how it will work but we'll see as we go along. In the meantime, as I said earlier, I've got a bit of leeway to make up and I shall need all your support. We shall have the eyes of the whole Submarine branch on us the whole time, but I think with a bit of luck we should have a very good commission.'

The wardroom picked up their glasses again. Fair enough, they said to themselves.

2

Wilfred leaned over the after end of *Seahorse's* bridge, drew in a deep breath, and cupped his hands.

'*Midshipman!* What's happening down there? What's the delay?'

The Midshipman, very self-conscious in his brand-new yellow lifejacket, was still too new to have developed the submarine casing officer's superb disregard for the oaths and exhortations hurled at him from the bridge. He looked up nervously.

'Just coming in now, sir,' he said.

'Well chop chop! We were supposed to be singled up five minutes ago.'

'Aye aye, sir.' The Midshipman turned to the leading seaman in charge of the party on the after casing, a squat, swarthy man named Gorbles who wore a prophet's beard and had been handling berthing wires on the casings of submarines for years.

'Can we hurry it up please, Gorbles?'

Leading Seaman Gorbles spat leisurely into the creek. 'All ready now, sir.'

The Midshipman relayed the news to the bridge and was rewarded by a furious scowl from Wilfred.

'Don't you worry about them up there, sir,' Leading

Seaman Gorbles said, confidentially. 'They got nothing better to do. You be like the Torpedo Awficer, sir. When they shouts at you, tell 'em to go and take a running poke at a rolling doughnut.'

Seahorse was ready for sea. Everyone was now waiting for The Bodger who, true to the tradition of submarine captains, was standing on the jetty, brief-case in hand, delaying going aboard his ship until the last moment.

An impressive committee had come to see The Bodger off, consisting of Captain S/M, Commander S/M, the duty staff officer, several heads of departments in the submarine depot, a few captains of other submarines, and a quartermaster with a bosun's call waiting to pipe The Bodger over the side. 'Sir Bedivere and friends,' said Dagwood, watching from the bridge.

The Bodger knew exactly why he had such a large and high-powered audience, gathered like vultures, to see him off. They were all curious to see how the new boy would shape. The Bodger suspected that they had all come half-hoping to witness a startling display of ship-handling. The Bodger could even see the figure of the Admiral, watching from his office window.

Commander S/M glanced at his watch. The other submarine captains assumed an expectant look. Captain S/M shook hands with The Bodger.

'Good luck, Bodger. It'll all come back to you.'

'Thank you, sir.'

The Bodger sensed the same expectancy when he reached *Seahorse's* bridge, where Wilfred, Gavin, Derek and Dagwood were waiting to report their departments ready for sea. The Bodger knew by their faces that they too were curious to see their new captain perform. Even the sailors busy taking in the gangplank, although they moved unconcernedly, were plainly conscious of a change of management. Down below, the control room watch devoutedly hoped that the new boss would not hit anything.

'Right, Number One,' said The Bodger. 'Let's go.'

Wilfred waved a nonchalant hand forward, and again aft. The breast ropes dropped. The Union Jack at the bows was struck. The Bodger seized his microphone.

'Slow astern port. Slow ahead starboard.'

The water whipped and frothed round the stern.

'Port screw going astern starboard screw going ahead sir,' intoned the Signalman. When the ship was manœuvring alongside, it was the Signalman's duty to stand at the back of the bridge and report to the Captain the actual—as opposed to the ordered—movement of the screws. It was not a part of his profession that the Signalman took seriously; he had long been convinced that nobody listened to a word he said. 'One of these days,' he frequently promised himself, 'I'll say, Both screws dropped off, sir, and I bet no *bastard* takes any —— notice.'

Seahorse's stern swung away from the jetty. The Bodger caught the swing and the submarine backed slowly out into the main harbour, the Signalman keeping up a steady monotone commentary. The committee on the jetty watched her go and then broke up, feeling vaguely cheated.

The Bodger could not have picked a more testing occasion for his first day. It was a fine sunny spring morning and everyone who had any business on the river was afloat. A dockyard tug shot across *Seahorse's* stern as The Bodger completed his turn. A ferry passed close down the starboard side as The Bodger was lining up his ship for the harbour entrance where, just outside on the western sand-bank, a dredger was lying half-way across the channel. A motor boat crammed with sightseers darted in front of *Seahorse's* bows as she picked up speed. The Bodger could hear the guide's voice over his loud-speaker.

'. . . Here we have a bit of luck, ladies. Here we have H.M.S. *Seahorse*, the Navy's latest submarine. You can see the ship's company all wearing life jackets in case the submarine sinks . . .'

Outside in the main channel, The Bodger twice had to slow down as sailing boats tacked across his bows.

'All right for some,' said the Signalman bitterly, as he watched a yacht glide by. 'Not like Jolly John, in Daddy's yacht here.'

By the time *Seahorse* cleared the outer buoy, The Bodger could feel sweat on his back, his legs were aching, and he realised with some surprise that his whole body had been fiercely tensed, with every muscle knotted, since *Seahorse* left her berth. When he came down from the bridge, leaving Gavin on watch, The Bodger felt as though he had run a Marathon.

'Coffee, sir?' said the Steward, as The Bodger sat down.

'That's the most civilised suggestion I've heard today.'

'Just coming up, sir.'

The Steward was the ship's company's equivalent of Gavin Doyle. He was a dramatically good-looking young man with curly blond hair and a dimple on his chin. His face had a quality of innocence which, framed in a sailor's uniform, made nine out of ten girls feel, as they expressed it in their letters, funny all over. The Steward's private mail was the largest of any on board and was almost entirely composed of letters written on green, pink, or pale blue paper, perfumed, and with crinkled edges. They earned for the Steward the nickname of Mr Wonderful and gave the ship's company, to whom Mr Wonderful passed most of his mail, some of their most enjoyable reading.

'What's the matter with that signalman?' The Bodger asked, as he stirred his coffee. 'He keeps muttering and grumbling in the background like a sort of Greek chorus.'

'He's in love with a policewoman, sir,' said Dagwood. 'He's taken her out every leave for two years and last leave he tried to kiss her. Apparently she immediately seized him in a sort of judo grip and nearly broke his back!'

The Chief Stoker appeared at the wardroom door. The Chief Stoker was a giant Irishman with a broad beaming red face. He weighed nearly eighteen stone and had a belly laugh which could tremble a glass of beer at ten paces.

'Trim's on, sir,' he said to Wilfred.

'Thank you, Chief Stoker.'

'That reminds me,' said The Bodger. 'In future, I want the trim put on before we leave harbour. And go to diving stations and open up for diving as soon as we get outside. Mid, you'd better go with the First Lieutenant and see how to open up for diving.'

Most of the machinery outside the engine room of the submarine was maintained by a tiny bald-headed man with huge projecting ears who was known by the traditional submarine title of the Outside Wrecker. The Outside Wrecker was a Lancastrian and leg-spinner for the ship's cricket team. He had a poor idea of any officer's knowledge, particularly non-technical officers, and when he walked through the submarine with Wilfred he leaped forward to check every valve and system himself, as though the First Lieutenant's touch would infect the metal.

'When yer openin' oop fer divin',' he told the Midshipman, 'yer gettin' the boat ready to dive. There're certain things which moost be open and others which moost be shut. If yer miss one out, she won't go down and if she does happen to go down, she won't coom oop!'

'I see,' said the Midshipman.

'. . . And if yer in any bloody doubt whether to open or shut it, fer Chris-sakes leave it shut.'

'I see.'

There was still one thing puzzling the Midshipman. He ventured to ask the Outside Wrecker.

'What's the trim, please?'

'It's what the Jimmy makes a balls oop of,' said the Outside Wrecker cryptically and sidled off towards the artificers' mess.

The Midshipman decided to put the same question to the oracle himself.

'Every time we go to sea,' said Wilfred, 'I work out a little sum about how heavy the boat is and how much water to have in the tanks. I give the figures to the Chief Stoker and he makes sure the right amounts of water are in the right tanks. That's what he means by "The trim's on".'

When they got back to the wardroom, The Bodger said: 'Mid, go up and relieve the Navigating Officer and dive the submarine when I tell you.'

'Aye aye, sir.' One of the cardinal rules drummed into the Midshipman as an ordinary seaman had been: 'Obey the order first, ask questions afterwards.'

Gavin was surprised to see him.

'Hello, old boy. Come up for a bit of freshers?'

'No, actually I've come up to relieve you.'

'Oh.' Gavin thought for a moment. 'Oh splendid. Well, let me see now. We're a mile inside the diving area, steering one-nine-four, both telegraphs half ahead, four hundred revolutions. Patrol routine, "Q" flooded, radar in the warmed-up state. Only one ship in sight, that's that one, and she's going away. O.K.?'

The Midshipman, to whom the traditional catechism of the officer of the watch's turnover was so much gibberish, swallowed and said: 'Yes, but I've got to dive the submarine!'

'Bully for you, boy. Don't pull the plug until I get down there, will you?'

'No, I won't, I promise.'

Gavin softened. 'D'you know how to do it?'

'I-I haven't the faintest idea.'

'It's not all that difficult. When the Boss tells you to dive the boat, all you've got to do is tell the look-out to clear the bridge, shut the voice-pipe cock, take a quick look round to see if you haven't missed anything and then climb into the hatch yourself. Just on your right you'll find a little tit. That's the diving klaxon. Press the tit twice. You must do it twice. If you only do it once nothing'll happen. Then all you've got to do is shut the hatch before the cruel sea comes in. Got that?'

'Yes, I suppose so.'

'Right. It's all yours. Don't look so *worried*, boy. You've got lots of time. This boat takes so long to dive you've got time to walk round the bridge and have a quick drag after the main vents open. Don't forget, *two* presses on the tit.'

'No. I mean . . . yes.'

Gavin disappeared and the Midshipman was left in command. He looked about him as though he expected the gigantic bows of a liner to crash into the submarine at any minute. But, as Gavin had indicated, the horizon was almost empty. The Isle of Wight lay far astern. A fresh wind was blowing from the south-west. There was no swell, only short waves with plenty of white horses to hide the feather of a periscope. It was, though the Midshipman could not appreciate it, perfect submariner's weather.

'Nice day, sir, isn't it?' the look-out remarked conversationally.

The Midshipman noticed the look-out for the first time. He was a young sailor in a duffle coat and a woollen ski-cap on which 'Ripper' was embroidered. He had a perky, Cockney face which suggested costermongers' barrows, programme sellers at Lords and jellied eels.

'Yes it is,' said the Midshipman.

'This your first submarine, sir?'

'Yes.'

'It's a *hell-ship*, sir,' said Ripper earnestly.

'*Is* it?'

'I should say so. It's . . .'

'*Midshipman*,' The Bodger's voice crackled over the broadcast. '*Dive off the klaxon!*'

While the Midshipman remained paralysed, Ripper leaped round the bridge, shut the voice-pipe cock, collected the binoculars and vanished inside the tower. All at once the Midshipman found himself alone, the last man on the bridge of a submarine about to dive. It was the loneliest moment of the Midshipman's life.

The klaxon button was where Gavin had described it. The Midshipman pressed it twice and far below, as though on a different planet, he heard its sound in the control room. At once, there was a roar of escaping air from outside the submarine, the engines stopped, and there was silence, in which the Midshipman could hear his breath rasping through his throat as he struggled with the top hatch.

The hatch would not budge. In a frenzy the Midshipman seized the handle and pulled with all his strength. The hatch swung shut with a violence which knocked the Midshipman off balance. One of the clips removed his hat and dealt him a stunning blow on the head. He had not been prepared for the complete blackness when the daylight was shut out and he hung on the ladder, unable to see, dazed by the blow on the head, incapable of finding the clips and appalled by the thought of the sea by now rising steadily up the outside of the tower.

'Here, sir.'

The Midshipman felt Ripper's hands guide him to the clips. He tightened them and slipped in the securing pins.

The Bodger was already at the periscope when the Midshipman reached the bottom of the ladder.

'Well done, Mid,' The Bodger said, without looking up. 'Bloody good for the first time.'

Standing at the bottom of the ladder, rubbing the bump on his head, the Midshipman experienced a soaring exaltation of his spirit; he felt, for the first time, a proper member of the ship's company. The Midshipman in that moment, was unwittingly bitten by the submariner's disease. It was an affliction which would remain with him all his life and would make him run to the rail whenever he saw a submarine pass by and stand a-tiptoe when they were named.

The day's dive was The Bodger's first opportunity to put his new ship's company through their paces and it took the ship's company only a short time to realise that they had taken on board a Caesar. Standing in the control room while his ship's company raced round him, The Bodger took his ship and made it jump through hoops. They practised putting out a fire in the main battery and

29

restoring electric power by emergency circuits. They exercised the hydroplanes and the steering gear in emergency control. The Chef was required to put out a fire in his galley. The engine room staff rigged emergency methods of pumping and flooding. The Steward steered the ship, while the Coxswain operated the switches in the motor room. The Chief Stoker and his store-keeper, a lanky, saturnine stoker called Ferguson, laboured to bring up fantastically-shaped pieces of spare gear which had not seen the light since the day they were installed. After two hours of it, the ship's company felt as though they had been put through a wringer.

'If this submarine was an animal,' said Leading Seaman Gorbles, 'we'd have the R.S.P.C.A. after us.'

'Keep silence,' said the Coxswain.

'Aye aye, Swain,' said Leading Seaman Gorbles.

Leading Seaman Gorbles disliked the Coxswain. Most of the ship's company disliked the Coxswain but not because he was the ship's master-at-arms and responsible for disciplinary matters, nor because he was also the ship's catering officer and responsible, under the First Lieutenant, for the amount and variety of the sailor's food. Other submarine coxswains suffered under these disadvantages and still remained popular and respected men. It was not in his professional but in his private life that the Coxswain offended. The Coxswain had, in the distant past before he became a Coxswain, got religion. The normal submarine sailor regarded religion as something to be used when strictly necessary, at its proper time and in its proper place, classifying it in the scale of usefulness after Eno's Salts but before an appendectomy. They mistrusted anyone except a padre who looked upon it in any other light. It was perhaps this mistrust which led to a poem being pinned on the control room notice board on the day *Seahorse* commissioned which defined the ship's company's attitude to their Coxswain.

> 'This is the good ship *Seahorse*,
> The home of the bean and the cod:
> Where nobody talks to the Coxswain,
> Cos the Coxswain talks only to God.'

When *Seahorse* surfaced after her day's exercise, The Bodger felt as invigorated as though he had just had a cold bath and a massage. He knew now that he had the structure and potential of a very good ship. All that was needed was to breathe it into life. He was also selfishly pleased with his own performance. He had gained in confidence with each minute. The old commands, the familiar submarine street-cries, had all come back to him, as Captain S/M had predicted they would. Having laid his first foundation, he could safely pass on to the next item.

'*Now*,' he said, rubbing his hands. 'Let me see some of the correspondence.'

Rusty, who was the ship's correspondence officer, guiltily brought out a file marked 'Captain to See.' The worst moment of any submarine correspondence officer's day was the moment when the Captain called for the correspondence pack. It nearly always meant trouble for someone.

'Yes,' said The Bodger doubtfully. 'The one I'd like to see is the 'Captain *Not* To See' pack. I always had one when I was Black Sebastian's correspondence officer. Who on earth are the EetEezi Catering Company?'

'They supplied the food during our contractor's sea trials, sir,' said Rusty.

'Why have we got a letter from them still in here? Ditch it. What's this *gauge* all this stuff is about?'

'It's a gadget for the distiller, sir,' said Derek.

'Have you all seen it?'

'I think so, sir.'

'Well, take all this rubbish away and put it in your own pack. I don't see anything about this place we're supposed to be going to tomorrow?'

'I've made a special pack for that, sir.'

Rusty handed The Bodger a bulky pack marked 'Oozemouth—For Sunny Holidays.'

The Bodger rubbed his chin. 'I see we're open to the public every day from two to six. Is that O.K. with you, Chief?'

'It should be, sir,' said Derek. 'We haven't got anything big on, unless something expensive happens on the way there.'

'Good. I don't see any visits from schools or sea cadets here?'

'We haven't fixed that yet, sir.'

'That *must* be done, right away. We'd better have a Schools Liaison Officer. Dagwood . . .'

'Sir?' said Dagwood, apprehensively.

'. . . You've been selected from a host of applicants. As soon as we get there, I want you to go ashore and ring up every school in the place and ask them if they'd like to send a team down. Ask them all—sea cadets, girl guides, Band of Hope—everybody. Give the local crèche a ring, too. They may have some embryo submariners for all we know. This is supposed to be a flag-showing visit and we're going to show the flag if it kills us. I don't give a damn about the general public. They've all seen too many gloomy films about submarines and they're only coming to satisfy their morbid curiosity. But the schools are a different thing. Unbelievable though it may be, that's the Navy of the future you're looking at, under that disgusting school cap and behind those indescribable pimples. You give a boy a good time when he comes to visit your boat and he'll remember it all his life. So schools and sea-cadets are the number one priority, no matter when they want to come and no matter how many they want to bring. They won't want very much, no detailed descriptions or anything like that. Just being in a submarine will be enough. And if they don't give the ship a cheer when they leave you can take it that the visit's been a failure. So don't forget. It's Billy Bunter, Just William and the Fifth Form at St. Dominic's we're after. Mum, Dad, and Uncle Henry can look after themselves. It'll need a bit of organising, Dagwood. We don't want them all at once and yet we don't want the boat looking like a Giles cartoon twenty-four hours a day for six days. Think you can do it?'

'Oh yes, sir.'

'I'm told we'll have some boffins, too, from some Admiralty Research Establishment or other. You'd better deal with them, Chief. They're the worst of the lot, of course, but go easy with them. They've been sitting on chairs so long the iron has entered their souls.'

Dagwood relished the last remark on the boffins. He had been a little overpowered by The Bodger's speech on Billy Bunter *et al.* but now he was relieved, and delighted, to see in The Bodger the gleam of a dry sardonic sense of humour.

'Have we got a press hand-out?'

'Yes, sir. S/M had a couple of thousand run off before we left.'

'Has it got a photograph?'

'Yes, sir.'

'Splendid.' The Bodger began to turn over the papers in the 'Oozemouth' pack. 'Football against the police. Cricket against the fire brigade. Badminton against King William IV Grammar School. Visit to a brewery. Visit to a chemical works. Visit to an oil refinery. Reception in the Mayor's parlour. Free tickets to *We Couldn't Wear Less* at the Intimate Theatre. Darts against the "Drunken Duck." We're going to have our work cut out, men.'

As The Bodger sifted through the invitations, he began to understand that the City of Oozemouth had exerted itself to be hospitable. There were honorary memberships of yacht clubs, tennis clubs and golf clubs; free tickets for plays, concerts and dances; and a card for every member of the ship's company entitling him to travel free in municipal transport when in uniform.

'What's this, supper and classical records with the Misses English-Spence, for two sailors? Have we got any classical music fiends, Dagwood?'

'I think the Radio Electrician and the Chef know a bit about it, sir.'

'The Chef! Good God! Well, there we are. Obviously we're going to have to wave the old flag until we drop. What time do we get there, Pilot?'

'Nine o'clock tomorrow morning, sir,' said Gavin.

At nine o'clock, in a light drizzle of rain, *Seahorse* reached the fairway buoy and passed up the channel to the City of Oozemouth. In spite of the rain, they were cheered all the way up. The main road which ran close to the water's edge for part of the way was packed with drenched holiday-makers. People perched on the roofs of cars and leaned from windows to wave. The inner harbour was swarming with sailing boats and pinnaces. *Seahorse's*

34

black hull moved among them like a shark's fin in a shoal of minnows. A sodden sea cadet band was playing on the jetty as *Seahorse* secured.

'Zero hour,' said The Bodger. 'Synchronise your watches, men.'

3

'But don't you get terrible claustrophobia?'

'No ma'am, only thirsty.'

'But I thought you got rum?'

'Yes ma'am, but not enough.'

H.M.S. *Seahorse* was open to the public for the first day and the citizens of Oozemouth were determined to make the most of the first submarine to visit their city since the day the war ended, when a German U-boat stupefied the local coastguards by surfacing next to the fairway buoy and hoisting a white flag. A squad of policemen with linked hands held back a surging, thrusting mass of holiday-makers, sea-cadets, tradesmen and seamen from neighbouring merchantships. Behind the public, mustered in ominous phalanxes, were the First Seven Schools.

Dagwood had spent a lurid two hours on the port harbour-master's telephone immediately *Seahorse* had secured. He had discovered that there were forty-two educational establishments in Oozemouth and district, ranging in size and denomination from Oozemouth Secondary Modern School, with over a thousand pupils, to Miss Elizabeth Warbeck's Academy for Daughters of Gentlewomen in Reduced Circumstances, with ten girls.

Bearing in mind The Bodger's strictures on the subject of Billy Bunter, etc., Dagwood had telephoned them all and every school had said it would like to bring all its pupils. Dagwood had made a swift calculation. Forty-two schools, in six days, made seven schools a day.

The First Seven Schools had arrived and were being held back by the brute force of the police, assisted by depressed-looking men in faded sports-coats and ginger moustaches and large women in tweed suits and pork-pie hats, who were circulating amongst the tide of coloured school caps, squashed velour hats, satchels, hockey-sticks, and straw boaters like cow-hands at a round-up. A gigantic nun, wearing a headdress reminiscent of the Medici, was laying about her with an implement which seemed to The Bodger, watching in horrified fascination from *Seahorse's* bridge, to be a crozier. Hats, caps and satchels were falling into the harbour in a steady rain and were being retrieved by an old man in a blue sweater and three days' growth of white stubble. The old man had not had such a day in his small boat since the time the brewer's lighter came apart at the seams and four dozen barrels of assorted beers went floating out on the ebb tide.

When, suddenly, the Seven Schools broke through the police cordon and swept towards the gangway, the Bodger hurriedly left the bridge and went down to the wardroom where he poured himself a stiff whisky and followed it with another. The only other person in the wardroom was Gavin, who was pretending to study a chart.

'What are you doing, Pilot?' The Bodger asked him.

'Sailing plan for Exercise Lucky Alphonse, sir.'

'Never mind about that just now. Get up top and start showing people round.'

37

'Yes, sir.'

Shortly there were shrill screams from forward, where Gavin had run into a party of girls from the Secondary Modern School.

Left alone, The Bodger was settling down to enjoy his whisky when he became aware of a rich north country voice resounding from the control room outside.

'Bah goom,' said the voice, 'Ah wish Ah had a quid for every time Ah've whanked one of these.'

Cautiously, The Bodger peered round the corner of the wardroom door.

The speaker was a tubby cheerful-looking little man in a brand-new checked sports coat and a blue shirt open at the neck. With him was a lady who was plainly his wife and there were four children, two girls who looked like their father and two boys who resembled their mother, standing in a row which reminded The Bodger of a cocoa advertisement. It was clear that the tubby little man needed nobody to show him around. He was fingering the shining handles lovingly and passing his hands knowingly over the air valves. He sniffed, and a delighted smile of nostalgia spread over his face.

'Eeh, it hasn't changed a bit! Diesel an' cabbage an' sweat!'

'*Bert*,' said the wife.

'Maria, Ah was in these things for four years before Ah married you an' they were the best years of mah life. Ah was Outside Wrecker and Ah remember one day off Sicily we 'ad something loose in the casing an' the Captain asks for volunteers to go and fix it. So the Engineer and me goes up and fixes it. When we got down again the Captain said to me, Biggs, he said, thart a brave man, Biggs. If an aircraft'd come while ther were up there Ah'd have to have dived without you. And Ah said, No tha wouldn't, Ah shut off t'panel afore Ah went, tha *couldn't've* dived. He just looks at me and when we got back he recommends me for warrant officer!'

The Bodger enjoyed the story. It had timing, punch, and a moral. Just as The Bodger was returning to his whisky he heard a small girl who was being held up to the after periscope by her mother squeal: 'Look mum, it's in technicolor!'

A black scowl wiped away The Bodger's indulgent smile.

Up on the casing, in steady rain, Petty Officer Humbold, the Second Coxswain, was showing a party of the general public round the upper deck. The painting and care of the outside of the submarine were the Second Coxswain's own particular responsibility. He was the Torpedo Officer's right-hand man when the submarine was entering or leaving harbour. He was a broad-shouldered, bullet-headed man with a torpedo beard and a pugnacious manner, as though he might at any moment punch his audience on their respective noses.

'Up there,' said the Second Coxswain, pointing at the gangling figure of Ferguson, the Chief Stoker's store-keeper, who was standing in oil-skins, boots and gaiters by the forward gangway, 'we have a sailor who's known as the Trot Sentry.'

The small band of the general public gazed at Ferguson, who was alternately blowing on his hands and making marks in a saturated note-book to note the number of visitors boarding the ship.

'He ain't good-looking, but like me and unlike you he's only here because he's gotta be.'

'Why haven't you got a gun?' asked a tall pale man in a cloth cap and a plastic raincoat.

'Can't afford one,' said the Second Coxswain shortly.

'Forrard, we have the anchor and cable. We've got one capstan, that's that little drum . . .'

'What's your job in this submarine, mister?' asked a youth in a black leather jacket and a crash-helmet.

'When the submarine dives, I run forrard as fast as I can and hold its nose. Back here, we've got the tower, where the awficer of the watch keeps 'is lonely vigil . . .'

'Don't you get claustrophobia in a submarine?'

'Only when I laugh,' said the Second Coxswain grimly.

In the engine room, Derek was entertaining the party of boffins. The Admiralty Research Establishment had provided an assorted collection of representatives, who were led by a senior scientist. There were four physicists, two marine biologists, three metallurgists, a specialist in wave formations, and a visiting professor from Harvard.

Derek led the way on to the engine room platform. In front of them were two panels of gauges, one for each engine, and all about them were the valves and systems for starting, controlling and stopping the engines. The party looked around in silence for a few moments.

'Holy Cow,' said the visiting professor from Harvard, at last. 'Rock-crushers!'

Derek bristled. He had cherished these engines from their earliest days. He had watched them grow from bare skeleton frames, lying on a shop floor, to thundering monsters capable of driving the submarine across the world.

'They're a little more than that,' he said coldly.

'Tell me,' said the Senior Scientist, 'do you go everywhere dived?'

'No. When we're on passage we go on the surface. In peacetime anyway.'

'Do the engines give you much trouble?' asked one of the metallurgists.

'Only when the Chief E.R.A. has a wash.'

'I beg your pardon?'

'It seems to be traditional that the Chief E.R.A. of a submarine never washes at sea. If he does, something goes wrong with the engines to get him dirty again.'

The Wavemaker looked at the tangle of pipes around him.

'How do you figure out all these pipe systems? They don't seem to lead anywhere.'

'Actually, these systems are better than most,' Derek said. 'They've been planned on a mock-up first, before they were ever put into a submarine. Most submarine systems look as though they were designed by Salvador Dali. Of course, they were put in under the old Olympic System.'

'The *Olympic* System?' The Senior Scientist shook his head.

'The fastest dockyard matie won, sir. Every morning while the submarine was building the men from the various dockyard departments lined up on the dockside holding their bits of pipe. Then when the whistle blew they all doubled on board and the man who got there first had a straight run. The others had to bend their pipes round his. The beauty of the system was that it didn't matter what size the pipes were. If the electrician was particularly agile he could put his bit of quarter-inch electric cable in first and watch the boiler-maker bend his length of eight-inch diameter special steel piping round it.'

'*Really?*' said the Senior Scientist.

'Yes,' said Derek, looking the Wavemaker, who appeared to be sceptical, defiantly in the eye. 'Now, gentlemen, was there anything in particular you wished to see?'

One of the physicists had a special request.

'May we see the distiller, please? I've been designing a special gauge for them and I would love to see where it's actually got to go.'

Derek showed them the distiller. The Physicist was thrilled.

'I'm *so* glad we saw that,' he said. 'Do you know, I've been designing them, and writing letters about them, and giving advice about them for a long time and this is the first time I've actually seen one!'

Good God, Derek said to himself.

'How stable are these boats in rough weather?' the Wavemaker asked.

'Pretty good. The fin keeps them more or less dry, not like the older boats with low towers. The stability has to be pretty carefully worked out, of course. We do a trim dive in the dockyard basin after every refit. Occasionally they make a mistake. One boat I went to sea in very nearly capsized. We heeled over to about fifty degrees and stayed there. I thought we'd all had it.'

'Of course,' said the Wavemaker, 'in a case like that we've got to differentiate between actual *danger*, and mere *discomfort*.'

Derek ground his teeth and repressed an almost overwhelming urge to howl out loud.

'Now, is there anything else, gentlemen?'

The Senior Scientist looked sheepish.

'I wonder . . .'

'Yes, sir?'

'I wonder. . . . It seems silly but . . . I wonder if you could explain something I've always been puzzled about . . .'

'Yes, sir?'

'How exactly does a submarine dive?'

'Well sir, all along the outside of the boat we've got a

row of very large tanks, called main ballast tanks. They're open to the sea at the bottom and closed at the top by very large valves, called main vents. When we open the main vents, the sea rushes in at the bottom and the air rushes out at the top, the submarine in effect shrinks in volume, displaces less water and therefore becomes heavier and therefore sinks. When we want to come up again we shut the main vents and blow the water out with compressed air. That makes the boat sort of swell again, displaces more water, become in effect lighter, and up she comes again. All done by Archimedes' principle, sir.'

'Archimedes?'

'You remember the chap, sir,' said the Wavemaker. 'He lived in a barrel.'

'Ah yes,' said the Senior Scientist.

In the control room, the Schools Liaison Officer was explaining technical matters to a crowd of schoolboys. Keep it simple, The Bodger had said. Dagwood began his address on first principles.

'These levers raise and lower the periscopes, and these open and shut the main vents. The main vents are . . .'

'Solenoid-operated, I suppose?' said a treble voice, casually.

'Huh?' Dagwood was thrown out of his stride. 'As a matter of fact, they are. This is the starter for the L.P. Blower . . .'

'It puts the final bit of air into the ballast tanks after surfacing,' said another treble voice confidently. 'Naturally you wouldn't use air from the bottles for all of it. You would use only enough to get you to the surface. H.P. Air is too precious in a submarine.'

Dagwood felt the hair on the back of his neck prickle with the first cold feeling of foreboding.

'Quite right,' he said. 'Now this . . .'

43

'The Germans used to use the exhaust gases from the engine starting instead.'

'*Did* they?' said Dagwood.

'Yes.'

A very small boy whose face was almost entirely extinguished by hair and by an enormous blue school cap said: 'What would you do if the submarine began to drop towards the bottom, sir?'

Dagwood thought rapidly.

'I would go hard a port, or hard a starboard, and full astern. That would tend to bring the bows up.'

'And if that didn't work, sir?'

'Blow the forrard main ballast tank.'

'And if that didn't work?'

'Blow *all* main ballast tanks.'

'And if that didn't work?'

Dagwood had by now the attention of everyone in the control room; there was a hush as they waited for his answer.

'That would work all right,' he said finally. But he did not feel that he had convinced anybody.

Far aft in the after torpedo space, Leading Seaman Miles, the torpedo rating in charge of the compartment, was being asked the same question by another schoolboy.

'What would you do,' the questioner's voice was charged with drama, '*if the submarine began to hurtle towards the bottom of the sea completely out of control?*'

'Face aft and salute, lad,' said Leading Seaman Miles easily.

Just aft of the control room, Leading Seaman Gorbles was explaining a delicate point to two schoolmasters.

'These are heads. What you call lavatories. There's one for the officers, one for the petty officers and one for the sailors. That's democracy.'

One of the schoolmasters had a dim memory connected with submarine toilets.

'Are they easy to work?'

'Dead easy. You just flush 'em. In the old days it was a bit tricky, you had to blow 'em over the side. You had to ring up the control room and ask the awficer of the watch before you did it. We used to get fed up with that rigmarole after a bit so we used to ring up and say: "Shit?" and they said: "Shoot!" '

In the fore ends, the Midshipman was explaining the escape system to Miss Elizabeth Warbeck, her niece Miss Sarah Warbeck, and the ten daughters of gentlewomen in reduced circumstances. Miss Elizabeth Warbeck was a tiny but staunch lady, with the perky air of a gamecock. Her eyes were sharp and interested in all she saw, her cheeks were rosy and her silver hair was drawn into a bun. The ten daughters of gentlewomen in reduced circumstances were uniformly dressed in grey tunics and berets.

But the Midshipman was chiefly interested in Miss Sarah Warbeck. He had first seen her, or rather a part of her, when she came down the fore hatch. The Midshipman had then discovered one of the least-publicised advantages of a submariner's life. No matter how tight her skirt nor how circumspectly she lowered herself, a girl descending through the fore hatch of a submarine was forced to display her legs.

The Midshipman had tactfully averted his eyes but could not prevent himself seeing enough of Miss Warbeck to whet his interest.

'This is an escape hatch,' he said. 'This is where you see John Mills and Co looking terribly brave on the movies. You let this trunking down and flood up the compartment until the pressure inside is equal to the sea pressure outside. Then you can open the hatch and duck under the trunking and go on up to the surface.'

The Midshipman paused and glanced quickly at his audience to see how they were taking it. He was gratified by Miss Sarah Warbeck's solemn expression.

'Of course in wartime,' he went on, 'all this would be removed to save weight and the hatches would be secured from the outside with clips.'

'But that's not fair!' said Sarah Warbeck indignantly.

The Midshipman gave a sad shrug, as though to say, That's the way the ball bounces.

'They have to be secured otherwise depth charges might blow them open. And anyway there wouldn't be anyone there to pick you up even if you did escape.'

'I think that's a swindle!' said Sarah Warbeck hotly.

The Midshipman gave another shrug, as though to say, Ah well, that's the way the cookie crumbles.

'Shall we look at the rest of the submarine?'

On their way they passed Gavin and a party of prefects from a girls' grammar school. The prefects were fully-developed wenches, under their school tunics. Gavin was having difficulty in keeping them to the point.

'This is the Petty Officers' Mess,' he announced.

'Is this where you live?'

'No, I live in the wardroom. The Coxswain lives here, and the Chief Stoker and . . .'

'Ooooh, do look at the beds, darling . . .'

'*Bunks*, Maureen darling . . .'

'Not very big, are they?'

'Not big enough for two, *darling* . . .'

'. . . And the Stoker Petty Officer and the Second Coxswain . . .'

'It's a good job you're all *men!*'

'Do you ever get kleptomania?'

'*Claustrophobia*, dar*ling.*'

'Barbara, you coarse thing!'

'. . . And the Electrical Artificer and the Radio Electrician and the Torpedo Instructor . . .'

'Who was that *gorgeous* man in white tabs . . .'

The gorgeous man in white tabs was enjoying the effect his remarks were having on Miss Elizabeth Warbeck and her niece. Their minds were now filled with pictures of black swirling water, explosions, feeble lights, and men struggling for breath. Miss Elizabeth Warbeck looked with compassion upon the Midshipman; he seemed so young to die.

They visited the galley next. The Chef was there in person, splendidly dressed for the occasion in a white apron and a tall white hat. The Midshipman was thankful that the Chef was not wearing his usual working rig of football shorts and bare chest, because the Chef was luridly and comprehensively tattooed. His tattoos included the words 'Mild' and 'Bitter', one over each nipple, and a dotted line round his throat, inscribed 'Cut here'. He also had an assortment of sailing ships, dragons, butterflies, crossed swords, naked women, and 'Mother' in a halo of laurel leaves, on his arms.

'Where did you get all those tattoos?' asked Miss Elizabeth Warbeck.

'Hong Kong, ma'am, Singapore, Yokohama, all over the place, ma'am.'

'I think they're terrific,' said Miss Elizabeth Warbeck warmly. The Chef was charmed. He showed them over his tiny galley.

'How many chefs do you have on board?'

'Only me, ma'am.'

'Only one Chef? For how many men?'

'Nearly seventy, ma'am.'

47

'Good gracious!'

All day long the noise of battle rolled in *Seahorse's*
passageways and living spaces. The general public tramped
determinedly through, fingering, pointing, gazing through
the periscopes, and exclaiming to each other at the
marvels they saw. On the jetty, a queue a quarter of a mile
long awaited their turn. Derek, who was duty officer, sat
in the wardroom feeling like a goldfish in a bowl and
trying to ignore the whispers and the shuffling feet behind
him. At last he was driven to his bunk and he lay there
with his curtain drawn. But the more curious members of
the public ventured into the wardroom, pulled the curtain
aside, and peered at him. Derek ignored them and concentrated on his book. It was a submarine story, just
published, by a popular writer of novels.

'A submarine in harbour,' Derek read, 'is a lifeless, dead
thing. It lies quiet, waiting, but with the hidden menace
of a sheathed sword . . .'

4

The first comedian was a bulky man in a pale blue suit which hung baggily from his shoulders.

'A funny thing happened to me on the way to the theatre tonight!'

The second comedian was a thin man in a pale green suit gathered very tightly at the waist.

'A funny thing happened to you on the way to the theatre tonight?'

'Yes. I met a man who had fourteen children!'

'You met a man who had fourteen *children?*'

'He said his wife was deaf!'

'He said his wife was *deaf?*'

'Yes. Every night he said to her, Shall we go to sleep, dear, or what?'

'Ha! Every night he said to her, Shall we go to sleep, dear, or *what?* Go on, Jimmy.'

'I'm goin' on. And every night she said, What?'

'Ha ha! Every night she said, What? Ha! Smashin' audiences you get here in Oozemouth, eh Jimmy? Smashin' audi . . .'

'I fell out of my bloody cradle laughing at that one!' shouted a voice from the dress circle which Gavin, sitting in the front row of the stalls, recognised as that of Leading Stoker Drew, of H.M.S. *Seahorse.*

49

'Turn it up, mate,' said Jimmy. 'I wouldn't knock the broom out of your hands if you were working. Did I ever tell you the one about the old lady who saw an elephant eating cabbages in her front garden, 'Arry?'

'No, Jimmy, you never told me the one about the old lady who saw a *hephalump* eating cabbages in her front garden . . .'

The Intimate Theatre was an Edwardian relic. The gaslight had been superseded by electricity but the chandelier in the foyer, the red plush seats, the gilded scroll work along the rim of the dress circle and the engraved glass on the box office window still remained. The theatre was a period piece. As the 'Empire Palace,' it had billed Marie Lloyd and had staged the provincial runs of *Floradora* and *The Belle of New York* to packed houses. But the visitor in search of nostalgia would have been disappointed. The glory had long since departed. The stage of the Intimate Theatre was now inhabited by bored girls who exhibited their bodies on revolving pedestals for twelve pounds a week and by comedians who ground out jokes about sexual perversion. The theatre was due to become a supermarket at the end of the year.

Jimmy and Harry finished their patter. The orchestra struck up. Jimmy and Harry shuffled to the centre of the stage, sang two choruses of 'Underneath The Arches,' waited for applause and, disappointed, shuffled off. The orchestra struck up again. A line of chorus girls galloped on and began to swing their legs mechanically at the audience. Leading Stoker Drew gave an appreciative howl and was helped from the theatre by two large men in shirt-sleeves.

'What do you think, Rusty?' said Gavin.

'Pretty starved-looking lot. You can count the ribs on that end one.'

'I like the second one from the end, though. The small dark one.'

'What do you say then, shall we try back-stage?'

'We'll see. Getting back-stage in one of these places is like trying to break into the Kremlin. We'll have to play it off the cuff.'

Three hundred yards away from the Intimate Theatre, in the same street, The Bodger, Wilfred and Dagwood had disposed of the Mayor's clear soup and grilled sole and were preparing to attack the Mayor's roast duck.

The dinner for the Captain of H.M.S. *Seahorse* was a civic occasion. The City of Oozemouth had laid out its best dinner service, polished its best silver, chilled its best hock, warmed its best claret, and decanted its best port. The Mayor and Mayoress were there in person, supported by a goodly muster of aldermen and their ladies. The Bodger, for his part, had changed into mess dress with miniature medals and a clean white stiff shirt. He had also brought Wilfred and Dagwood as moral support.

'I've been to these things before,' he said to them, as they sat in the Mayoral limousine which was bearing them towards the Mayor's parlour. 'You'll get a first-class dinner and vino, but the conversation will drive you up the wall if you don't watch it. Do either of you know anything about boiling soap or smelting copper?'

'No, sir.'

'You will, by the end of this evening. That's the sort of thing these characters are pretty hot on. By the way, I've been boning up on a little local colour. Oozemouth United got to the semi-final of the F.A. Cup last year. The Oozemouth Festival Orchestra is second only to the

Liverpool Philharmonic amongst provincial orchestras, though you'd better say for the sake of argument tonight that it's the best. Oozemouth makes the best electric light bulbs in the world and remained loyal to the Crown during the Civil War. That's about all I've managed to pick up.'

'Thank you very much, sir,' said Wilfred and Dagwood gratefully.

After the initial commonplaces about the weather, the traffic, and the criminal financial policy of the government had been exchanged, it suddenly became clear that The Bodger had seriously misjudged the conversational range of his hosts. While The Bodger was shyly admiring the delicate colouring of the Goldbeerenauslese in his glass, the conversation took an unexpected and vaguely hostile turn.

'Commander,' said the Mayor. 'Tell me something I've always wanted to know about submarines.'

The Bodger composed himself to answer the usual chestnuts on claustrophobia and escape from sunken submarines.

'Why do men, like yourself for instance, go into submarines? What sort of man would do a thing like that?'

The cue was taken up at once by an alderman sitting further down the table whom The Bodger later discovered was the city's most prosperous undertaker.

'It is condemned in Holy Writ,' said the Undertaker stridently. 'Thou didst blow with Thy wind, the sea covered them: they sank as lead in the mighty waters. Exodus, fifteen, ten. And again,' the Undertaker's voice rose thrillingly, 'And their persecutors Thou threwest into the deeps, as a stone into the mighty waters. Nehemiah, nine, eleven.'

A ripple of agreement ran down the table.

'. . . Hear hear, Jeb . . .'

'. . . Took the words out of my mouth . . .'

'. . . Pure weapons of destruction, that's what they are . . .'

'. . . Should be banned . . .'

'Nasty underhand things,' said the Undertaker's wife.

Wilfred, sitting next to her, thought it time to change the subject.

'That was a jolly good show in the F.A. Cup last year,' he said, brightly, 'I mean, getting as far as the semi-finals . . .'

Wilfred's voice trailed away into silence when the Undertaker's wife looked at him.

The Bodger had been taken off guard by the unexpected and spiritually well-documented attack. He felt his way cautiously towards an answer.

'I don't know that it's up to me to say whether we should have submarines or not,' he said. 'The fact is, we've got them, everybody else who can afford them has got them, and lots of people who can't afford them would very much like to have them. As to why people go into submarines, that's very hard to answer. You might just as well ask why do people become missionaries or shop-lifters. I suppose the extra money has something to do with it but I'm sure that basically it all comes down to the question of which would you rather do, run your own firm, however small, or help to run someone else's, how-ever big. Would you rather be a small cog in a big machine or a big cog in a small machine. Most of our ship's company are big cogs in a small machine. They're nearly all specialists. They have clearly defined jobs and in most cases they're the only man for that job, although all of them can do the basic things in a submarine which everybody should be able to do. Take the chef as an example. His actual rate is Leading Cook. In a cruiser or an aircraft carrier he would probably be in charge of a watch of cooks, one cook in over a dozen. But in *Seahorse* he's not just *any* chef, he's *the* chef. He's one of the ship's personalities by reason of his job, if nothing else. Everyone in a submarine has a much greater *identity*, if you see what I mean, than his counterpart in general service. Everybody in a submarine has a much better idea of what's happening. In an aircraft carrier I don't suppose more than ten per cent of the men on board know what's going on at any given time. But in a submarine news goes round in a matter of minutes. The chart is on the chart-table in the control room most of the time. Anyone passing by can see where we are and where we're going.'

'Yes,' said the Mayor. 'Yes, I see what you mean, Commander. But I'm still of the opinion that it's a pity we have to make use of such things. I've never trusted all these new-fangled inventions . . .'

'Oh, but the *idea* of a submarine is not new at all, Your Worship,' said Dagwood, manfully stepping into the breach (while The Bodger thankfully resumed his meal; he had noticed that everyone else had already finished). 'It's true that the first really practicable submarine in the modern sense, the Holland boat, only went to sea at the beginning of this century. But Robert Fulton built a perfectly workable one during the Napoleonic Wars. And even earlier than that, at the beginning of the seventeenth century, a Dutchman called Cornelius van Drebbel made one which was propelled by oars. He even took King James the First down for a dive in it!' Dagwood warmed to his subject; he had done a deal of research into the history of submarines. 'Leonardo da Vinci had a design for a submarine . . .'

'Ah!' cried the Undertaker triumphantly. 'But he kept

it a secret, didn't he? He was afraid of the use evil men would put it to!'

'Yes, that's true,' Dagwood admitted, wishing he had never mentioned Leonardo da Vinci.

'And they besought him that he would not command them to go out into the deep. Luke, eight, thirty-one.'

'When are the Oozemouth Festival playing again?' Wilfred enquired of the alderman sitting opposite him.

'Which league do they play in, lad?'

While his seniors wrangled, the most junior member of *Seahorse's* wardroom was being very well entertained. Having dined very successfully *en famille* with Miss Elizabeth Warbeck and Sarah, the Midshipman had ventured to ask Sarah back to the submarine for a drink. To the surprise of them both, Miss Elizabeth Warbeck agreed.

Derek was very glad to see them. The public had gone, except for some odd pockets of sea cadets who were being mopped up by the duty watch. He was bored with his book (the hero's submarine was plunging, out of control, towards the bottom of the Timor Sea, the hero being baffled) and he was bored with being by himself while the rest were ashore.

Recognising the situation at a glance (Derek had been entertaining ladies in submarines while the Midshipman was still at his preparatory school), Derek knew exactly what was required of him. He opened a panel in the woodwork by his bunk and made a cunning two-way switch, installed by the builders at his personal request, which simultaneously extinguished the white lighting and replaced it with two dim red lights in opposite corners of the wardroom. He switched on Dagwood's tape recorder

which began to play soft dreamy music of the kind
defined by Dagwood himself as 'Eine Kleine Smooch
Musik.' Lastly, he opened the wine cupboard, took out
some bottles and clinked them invitingly.

'Chez Seahorse, we never closed,' he said to Sarah. He
was vastly taken with her. He admired the Midshipman's
taste.

'What'll you have?'

The Midshipman and Sarah were both a little taken
aback by the speed and facility with which Derek had
converted the wardroom into a very fair facsimile of a
sordid night-club.

'Well, I don't know what to have,' Sarah said. 'What
have you got?'

'Anything you like.'

'Except beer,' said the Midshipman.

'How about some Cointreau, Sarah?'

'Yes, that would be nice. But only a small one.'

'We don't have small ones here.'

Conversation came reluctantly at first, so reluctantly
that Derek had to work hard to keep it going; he began
to wonder indignantly why the Midshipman had bothered
to invite Sarah down to the boat at all. But after a time
the conversation started to flow freely, so freely that Derek
began to feel superfluous. When the Midshipman took
Sarah's hand and the conversation lapsed altogether
Derek wished that he could tactfully retire to bed. But
there was nowhere for him to go. Sarah was sitting on his
bunk.

Derek's dilemma was solved by the arrival of Gavin
and Rusty. They had succeeded in penetrating back-stage
at the Intimate Theatre and had carried off two members
of the cast, Gavin a brunette called Rita and Rusty a
large blonde called Moira.

56

Rita was one of the occupants of the revolving pedestals. She was twenty-eight and had been occupying pedestals, swings and window ledges in the nude since she came to London from her native Birmingham at the age of twenty. She had never been very intelligent academically but she had already sized up Gavin. His technique, which had laid waste so many hearts, rebounded from her as though from bloom steel. She had already made the decision not to make any decision about the evening's outcome but to wait and see.

Moira was a female xylophonist and a minor celebrity in the show, her name actually appearing on the bill, in the bottom right-hand corner. She might have been beautiful but for her size. She was like a good-looking girl seen through a magnifying glass. She was wearing a black satin skirt, a white nylon blouse through which a pink brassière was just visible, gipsy-dangle ear-rings, a jewelled Juliet cap and chunky wedge-soled sandals. She carried a red plastic handbag and exuded a musky scent which reminded Derek of magnolias and a heavy head-cold. She made herself at home at once.

'Oooh, this *is* nice! This *is* cosy. *Womb*-like, ain't it, Rita?'

'Yes,' said Rita shortly.

'Are you the captain?'

'No,' said Derek. 'I'm the engineer officer.'

'Oooh, I bet you're a clever chap. I'll have a drop of the Pope's telephone number, if you don't mind. With splash.'

'I'm sorry?'

'Vat 69, *dear*. You mustn't mind me, it's listening to Jimmy and Harry every night, you start to talk like them. Two shows a night, six nights a week, it's enough to send you screaming up the wall. It took my old man like that.

57

He's in a home now, you know. What's the captain like?'

'He's a very nice fellow,' said Derek.

'Where's he now?'

'Having dinner with the Mayor.' ·

'Ooooh, *posh.*'

Derek and Moira were left to carry on the conversation by themselves. The Midshipman and Sarah gazed at each other. Rusty said nothing. Gavin kept Rita under a steady predatory stare. Rita ignored everybody.

'I don't know how you find your way about one of these things, really I don't.'

'It's all quite logical when you know what to look for.'

'You clever thing!' Moira gave Derek a playful tap on the wrist which left him numb to the elbow.

'What do you do in the show, Rita?' said Sarah, suddenly.

'I pose in the nude,' said Rita, coldly.

'Oh.'

'Don't you mind her, dear.' Moira bent to whisper confidentially to Sarah. 'It's the *draughts!*'

When the taxi stopped outside her lodgings, Rita jumped out quickly.

'Thank you very much, Gavin,' she said. 'I've had a lovely time.'

'Will I see you again?'

Rita shrugged. 'Possibly,' she said distantly. 'Good night.'

Gavin watched her run up the steps, open the front door, and disappear.

'What happened, sir?' said the taxi-driver. 'Somebody bite her?'

When Moira's taxi stopped outside her door, she leaned over and kissed Rusty on the cheek.

'You're sweet. Are you married?'

'No.'

'Come up and have a cup of coffee.'

'Oh well, I don't . . .'

'Come *on*, I'm not going to bite you!'

Moira's room was at the top of the house. As they crept up the stairs, Moira said: 'Shush, don't wake my land-lady. I call her Exide. She keeps on after all the rest have stopped. Oh dear, there I go again.'

There was only one chair in the room and it was covered with clothes.

'You sit on the bed and I'll go down and get some coffee.'

Rusty sat down on the bed. After a few minutes' thought, he lay back and closed his eyes. It had been a long day. Rusty drew the counterpane up to his chin and fell asleep. When Moira came back, only the top of Rusty's head was visible above the counterpane.

'Cor Blimey O'Reilly, wakey wakey!'

Rusty stirred.

'Come on, just because you're a submariner you needn't stay submerged all the time!'

The night before *Seahorse* sailed from Oozemouth the wardroom gave a cocktail party to return hospitality. The Steward marshalled rows of bottles and glasses on the chart-table and donned a white coat himself. The Chef resumed his tall hat and fried six pounds of chipo-latas. The Petty Officer Electrician and his party rigged coloured lights along the casing. Miss Elizabeth Warbeck came during the afternoon and decorated the wardroom and the control room with flowers. The Mayor and Corporation attended with their wives and were followed after the last performance by the cast from the Intimate Theatre. The Midshipman and Sarah sat quietly in a corner of the wardroom. Jimmy and Harry pinned the Undertaker in a corner of the control room and told him jokes. Moira played 'When the Saints Come Marching In' on a line of glasses. The Mayor was heard to remark that submarines were a fine invention.

'In fact I'll go further, Commander,' he told The Bodger. 'We'll be damned sorry to see you go tomorrow.'

But when the morning came, it did not appear that *Seahorse* would go after all. A dense mist covered the harbour. Visibility was not more than a hundred yards. The mournful lowing of ship's sirens sounded through the fog. The Bodger would not normally have considered going to sea but there was another consideration.

'When have we got to be in position for "Lucky Alphonse," Pilot?'

'We're supposed to be dived in our area by noon tomorrow, sir.'

'How far have we got to go?'

'Almost four hundred miles, sir.'

'Well, we'll wait a little longer. When the sun gets up properly it may melt this lot away. I'll have another look at nine o'clock.'

At nine o'clock it seemed that the mist was thinning. The sun could be seen as a bright spot in the grey fog. The Bodger could see almost as far as the other side of the river. He decided to go to sea.

With radar operating, siren blasting and extra look-outs posted, *Seahorse* crept down harbour. Opposite the main road, where the channel narrowed, the fog clamped down more thickly than ever. The Bodger was forced to stop. He could not see *Seahorse's* casing from the bridge.

'What's the sounding now?'

'Four fathoms, sir. . . . Three and a half fathoms . . .'

'We must be getting damned close to that main road.'

'I think I can hear a car now, sir,' said Wilfred.

The Bodger listened intently. He was sure he could hear a car, too. His doubts were resolved a few moments later by the squealing of brakes, a tearing crash of metal and a loud splash.

The mist momentarily thinned and the men on *Seahorse's* bridge looked down upon a small green van which was submerged in water up to the windscreen. The driver was climbing out when he noticed *Seahorse* materialising out of the fog. He shook his fist and bellowed at The Bodger.

'My dear chap,' said The Bodger mildly. 'Hadn't you better start sounding your horn?'

5

Exercise 'Lucky Alphonse' was the biggest and most important fleet exercise of the year, being planned to last three weeks during which time one hundred and eighty ships of fourteen nations would steam over an area stretching from the Denmark Straits to the Canary Islands and four hundred and fifty aircraft would take off from airfields scattered between Dakar and Reykjavik. The villains, or attacking side, were Pink. The heroes, or defending side, were Blue.

'Just as I thought,' said The Bodger when he saw the Exercise Orders. 'Nuclear Cowboys and Indians.'

The Exercise Orders, when first issued, were thought to be a little too bulky, particularly for ships which had small operations rooms, but by brilliant cutting and inspired paraphrasing (at the risk of losing some of the nuances of the language) the Combined Staffs had succeeded in reducing the final edition to one more manageable volume equivalent in size, without Amendments, to the first two volumes of the London Telephone Directory. Amendments followed the Orders themselves at weekly intervals although many ships received the Amendments some weeks before the Orders. One destroyer from Rosyth received neither Orders nor Amendments but still acquitted herself with distinction in the Exercise; her Captain, a firm churchman, taking his part from the Second Book of Kings and Hymns Ancient & Modern.

When The Bodger received his copy he read the first page, where he noted the date the Exercise started, the last page, where he noted the date the Exercise finished, thumbed hopefully through the rest (once, as a young midshipman, The Bodger had come across a brand new ten shilling note in a copy of *Orders for Disabling Fleeing Luggers, Smacks & Jolly-Boats* published before the war), wrote 'Action—Navigating Officer' on the cover and then pitched the Orders on Gavin's bunk and forgot about them.

The ship's company, and the officers, had all done fleet exercises before. They knew the form: days of waiting, a few brief hours of excitement, and more days of waiting for the exercise to end, which it normally did twenty-four hours early because the planning staff had run out of incidents and wanted to catch the midnight train to London. But 'Lucky Alphonse', under The Bodger, was not just another exercise. The Bodger's drive began before *Seahorse* left harbour. The polished fittings on the bridge and the casing were painted black and the wires, guard-rails and ladders were landed. A full outfit of torpedoes was loaded and a false deck of stores laid out along the passageways. The periscopes were realigned, the torpedo tube firing mechanisms overhauled, and the radar sets recalibrated. When she finally left, *Seahorse* was stored for war.

When the ship was on patrol, The Bodger left nothing to chance. The submarine surfaced for nothing. The batteries were recharged by snorkelling and the rubbish which accumulated inside the submarine was fired into the sea through the gash ejector. The Bodger watched the smallest details, to the extent of personally supervising the weighting of the rubbish bags before they were ejected. 'I once followed a Yank submarine three hundred miles across the Arctic, just by the ice cream cartons,' he said.

The Midshipman was given a special job of his own.

'I want you to make out a Recognition crib, Mid,' The Bodger said. 'Get out *Janes Fighting Ships* and write down the tonnage, water-line length, funnel height and mast-head heights of every Blue ship in the exercise. When you've done that, write down by each ship any special features she may have. Almost every ship has something. The arrangement of the gun turrets, prominent radar aerials, lattice masts, cutaway quarterdecks, side lifts on the flight deck—anything I'll be able to recognise quickly through the periscope. Got it?'

'Yes, sir.'

The Midshipman sat down with *Janes Fighting Ships* and began work. It was only after The Bodger had left the wardroom that he ventured his question.

'Why am I doing this?'

'Recognition mostly,' said Gavin. 'And ranging. The Boss ranges on the heights of things. That's why he wants the height of funnels and radar aerials. He may be able to range on them when he can't see the actual mast itself.'

'Oh.'

The Midshipman returned to *Janes* with a renewed feeling that he was indeed a tenderfoot on a strange range. Hard though he tried to gain experience he was again and again reminded that he was now in a private world, incomprehensible to outsiders, demanding techniques and knowledge of its own. When the Midshipman tried to trim the submarine, for instance, his first attempts were disastrous.

64

'Have a go at the trim, Mid,' The Bodger said with a cheerful smile one morning when *Seahorse* had been on patrol for two days.

'Aye aye, sir.'

The Bodger remained in the wardroom, mentally crouched in the slips, his eyes fixed on the depth gauge and his finger-nails drumming on the wardroom table.

'There's only one way for the chap to learn and that's by doing it by himself,' said The Bodger to the rest of the wardroom, his face drawn in agony and his eyes straying again to the depth gauge. Almost at once he hit the control room deck at the double as the submarine, hitherto in perfect trim, responded to the Midshipman's tentative experiments by heading purposefully towards the bottom, a thousand fathoms below.

The rest of the wardroom were unnerved by the spectacle of their captain torturing himself in the sacred name of training. Wilfred, who was Trimming Officer and the most experienced trimmer in the ship, took it upon himself to give the Midshipman a special lecture on trimming.

'First of all,' he said, 'you've got certain things to help you trim. There's the depth gauge. That tells you how deep you are. There's the bubble on the inclinometer. That tells you whether you're level or not. And then there's the bathythermograph which tells you about the sea outside, but let's not worry about that for the time being. You've got two planesmen, to keep the boat at the right depth, and level. The ballast pump, to shift water into and out of the boat, and the trim pump which shifts water round and about the boat. You use all these things when you're trimming. There are people who can trim by the seat of their pants. They've been doing it so long they can tell what's wrong just by looking. But there's one sure-fire way anyone can use.'

'What's that?' the Midshipman asked, soberly conscious that he was being initiated into one of the world's obscurest sciences, a mystery understood only by a tiny number of people.

'Go to a hundred feet if you can, where it's relatively calm and peaceful. Slow down. Put the wheel amidships. Put the planes amidships. Then watch the depth gauge. If you're light, the boat will rise. If you're heavy, the boat will sink. So you pump or flood, using the ballast pump. Always get the bodily weight right first. Then watch the bubble on the inclinometer. If it runs forward you know you're light forrard and heavy aft. If it runs aft, you know you're heavy forrard and light aft. So you pump water whichever way you need with the trim pump. It's useful to remember, always pump towards the bubble. Eventually you should get to the state where the boat stays at the right depth and the bubble stays amidships, without using the planes. You see, you may have been keeping depth before but the planesmen may have been sweating blood to keep you there. What you're trying to do is to achieve a state of neutral buoyancy so that the boat has no tendency to go up or down.'

'Where does "Q" tank come in then?'

' "Q" has got nothing to do with the trim. It's either empty or full. It's an emergency tank which you flood when you want to go down in a hurry. Then you blow it out when you reach depth. The things that have an effect on the trim are the weight of fuel, water and stores, the number of people on board, the density of the sea water, and whether the boat is speeding up or turning under wheel or firing torpedoes. Even the weather up top has an effect down to a certain depth. Mind you, once

66

you've got a good trim that doesn't mean it'll last for ever. You might run into a patch of denser sea water, people move about, the weather might get a bit rougher. You've got to keep at it the whole time.'

'As well as looking through the periscope,' said The Bodger, who had been listening unobtrusively from the passageway. 'I'd rather you had a bloody awful trim and kept a good look-out.' The Bodger had been struck by a curious common factor in the reports of dived submarines which had collided with surface ships. In many cases the First Lieutenant, the Trimming Officer, had been on watch at the time of the collision and had been obsessed with the trim, taking a couple of gallons from one tank and putting a couple of gallons into another, while all the time the *Queen Mary* and the entire Home Fleet bore down on him at thirty knots.

The Midshipman took The Bodger's remarks to heart. He was indeed a little too zealous. The following afternoon the Midshipman was at the periscope by himself. It was the dead time of the afternoon. The planesmen yawned in their seats. Everyone except the watch was asleep. The Bodger himself was in his cabin, lightly dreaming of fat aircraft carriers steaming towards him on steady courses, when he was awakened by the sound of water flushing into 'Q' tank. The deck was tilting and the depth gauge already showed seventy feet.

'Six helicopters, sir!' cried the Midshipman.

The Bodger's eyebrows rose.

'*Six choppers!*'

Seahorse was three hundred miles from land and had met nothing but merchant shipping for three days.

'Have you blown "Q" yet?'

'Oh, no sir, I'm afraid.'

The depth gauge was showing a hundred and twenty

feet and the needle was still swinging rapidly. The Outside Wrecker, on the blowing panel, had the look of a man about to explode into a thousand pieces.

'Blow "Q". Sixty feet.'

At periscope depth again, The Bodger searched sea and sky meticulously.

'Damned if I can see any bloody choppers,' he growled.

The Bodger shook his head.

'Either you've got stereoscopic eyes or I'm going blind in my old age, Mid.'

'I'm very sorry, sir.'

'That's all right. You did the right thing. Always go deep for six choppers. Especially in the middle of the bloody Atlantic,' The Bodger added, to himself.

The Bodger left the periscope, climbed back into his bunk and composed himself for sleep. Just as he felt the warm comfortable recession of his senses, the deck tilted once more.

'They're back, sir.'

The Bodger gave the shame-faced Midshipman a curious look. Again he searched the sky. Again, he could see nothing but a wheeling seagull and the eternal grey waves rolling towards him at eye level.

'You feeling O.K., Mid?'

'Yes, sir. They're there, sir.'

'Oh, I'm sure they are.' The Bodger looked again. 'Ah . . . Wait, I see them. Is that them?' The Midshipman looked through the periscope and nodded. Flying steadily eastwards, looking neither to right nor left, were six large geese in line ahead.

The Bodger conceded that they did resemble helicopters to an untrained eye but the control room watch had not heard a better joke since the Coxswain got food poisoning. The helmsman tittered. The Outside Wrecker smirked. Ripper, on the foreplanes, grinned at his depth gauge. Even the Radio Electrician, a naturally sombre individual, sitting at the after planes, permitted himself a faint enigmatic smile.

'Never mind, Mid,' The Bodger said. 'Always go deep first and ask questions afterwards.'

Nevertheless, The Bodger could not avoid a feeling of disquiet. The affair of the Six Geese smacked suspiciously of bird-watching and bird-watching through the periscope was the submariners' traditional symptom of impending insanity. In The Bodger's experience, the feathered friends were normally followed closely by the men in white coats. The Bodger had once served with a captain who was actually murmuring: 'Strange to see black-backed gulls so far south' while a Japanese destroyer threshed past two hundred yards away. The Bodger resolved to keep a sharp eye on the Midshipman.

But when he had thought more deeply about the matter, The Bodger was not very surprised that the Midshipman should make mistakes on the periscope. The periscope was much more than a complicated optical instrument and to use it successfully required much more than mere good eyesight. A periscope demanded the ability to deduce facts from limited data, the ability to see a whole room through the keyhole, in short it demanded 'the periscope eye.' The task was hard enough in daylight. At night it was trebly difficult. Here again, the Midshipman provided the control room watch with some much appreciated entertainment.

The night following the affair of the Six Geese the Midshipman came on watch with Wilfred while the submarine was snorkelling to recharge the batteries. The Midshipman had no sooner taken over the periscope for the first time when he rang the 'Stop Snorting' Alarm and ordered 'Q' flooded. Once again, The Bodger tumbled out of his bunk.

'What's up, Mid? Luminous shite-hawks?'

'Aircraft dead ahead sir, coming straight towards!'

'Golly.' The Bodger scratched his head. 'Funny we didn't get any indication of it before. Was it lighted?'

'Very bright red light like a port wing light, sir.'

'Did you see anything, Number One?'

'No, sir.' Wilfred, too, was perplexed. It was a clear night with a sharply defined horizon and excellent periscope visibility. Surely he could not have missed a brightly-lighted aircraft?

'Well, we'll stay down for half an hour or so and see what happens.'

After half an hour The Bodger brought *Seahorse* back to periscope depth. As the periscope broke surface The Bodger swivelled round in a quick sweep.

'There's your aircraft, Mid,' he said, at once. 'It's Mars.'

The Midshipman blushed; what with flying geese and hostile planets, The Bodger must be beginning to think him a little touched in the head. But The Bodger seemed quite unconcerned about it.

'It's quite understandable,' he said. 'It's by far the brightest star in the sky and it could well be an aircraft light. Don't worry Mid, there's many a good submariner stopped snorting and gone deep for Mars or Venus, let me tell you. As I said before, I'd much rather you went deep unnecessarily a thousand times than stayed up once too often and got us clobbered by an aircraft. Go deep first, ask questions afterwards.'

The ship's company were grateful to the Midshipman. He provided them with almost their only source of innocent amusement as the days of the patrol crept by.

70

They had already settled to the strange twilight existence of a submarine on patrol. They slept through the day and came awake at nightfall for the one hot meal of the day which was normally cooked and eaten while the main engines were running to charge the batteries. Twice a day they went to maximum depth to take bathythermograph readings of the sea layers. The rest of the time was spent patrolling at periscope depth.

The passage of time was marked by the changing of the watches. Beards grew longer and more unkempt until the control room took on the appearance of a depression bread-line. The bread itself was harder and the slices grew smaller—as the crusts went mouldy and were cut off. The submarine ticked over in a somnolent state similar to a mass hibernation.

Seahorse's patrol position lay across a main shipping route and The Bodger stood at the periscope and watched the big tankers come up over the horizon, their huge slab sides and superstructures as big as blocks of flats gleaming white in the sunlight. The Bodger practised attacks on them. They made perfect targets, steaming on steady unalarmed courses, the massive hydrophone effect of their propellers pounding over *Seahorse's* sonar. They seemed quite unaware of a submarine's presence. If any of them ever noticed a suspicious flash from the sea as the sun caught the revolving glass of the periscope they showed no sign of it. Some of them passed less than a quarter of a mile from *Seahorse* and The Bodger was often unable to see anyone on watch on the bridge at all.

On the fifth day, The Bodger became concerned about the lack of contacts and moved to the extreme westward of *Seahorse's* area. The Bodger reasoned that the expected Task Force would assemble far out in the Atlantic to the westward and move eastward towards Ushant. A signal at midnight from ComSubPink confirmed The Bodger's theory. By dawn on the sixth day The Bodger was waiting on the westward edge of his area. It was, appropriately, the Midshipman who made the first sighting.

The Midshipman looked very closely before he mentioned it to Wilfred. He could not afford another mistake. If this turned out to be a fishing vessel or a floating spar of wood, he would never live it down.

'Number One, would you come and have a look, please? I think I can see the mast of a destroyer!'

Wilfred was at the periscope in one bound.

'O.K. I've got it. Call the Captain!'

The Bodger was delighted.

'That's well done, Mid. That's a good sighting. It's a destroyer all right, large as life. I can just see the tip of his funnel as well. We're fine on his port bow. No, he's just altered towards. But he's still a long way away. Number One, pipe "Attack team will be required in ten minutes' time".'

Leading Seaman Gorbles, the sonar watchkeeper, had been giving negative reports in a regular monotone voice. Suddenly, his voice went up a semitone.

'Possible H.E., bearing two-seven-zero. Faint transmissions on the bearing.'

The Bodger was jubilant. 'That's us! Blood for supper! Let's have a butchers.'

The Bodger took the second pair of earphones and listened as Leading Seaman Gorbles quartered the sea with sweeps of his set. The Bodger could hear the unmistakable throbbing of the destroyer's hydrophone effect, known in sonar parlance as 'H.E.', and the eerie pinging transmissions of its asdic set. Leading Seaman Gorbles had already begun his long recital of new hydrophone effects and bearing changes, couched in the esoteric dialect of the sonar world, which would continue until all the sounds had faded and the sea was empty once more.

'. . . H.E. louder, two-seven-two, moving right. Revolutions one-two-zero, classified turbine. Transmissions on the bearing, transmission interval varying. *Second* H.E., two-seven-nine, transmissions varying . . .'

The destroyers were still searching without contact. While their transmissions remained random and disconnected, a submarine could assume that it had not yet been detected. The Bodger went back to the periscope.

'It's them all right. I can see them now. It's two destroyers and there's something else behind them. . . . Can't see what it is, but it's a lot of ship! And *more* of them. . . . My God a whole bloody forest of masts! It's the Task Force, not a doubt about it.'

It was indeed the vanguard of the Task Force, spread out over a front of more than thirty miles. The Task Force had been assembling for the past two days, the earliest arrivals killing time in refuelling, carrying out asdic sweeps and narrowly avoiding collisions.

The main striking element of the Task Force was the two aircraft carriers H.M.S. *Great Christopher* and the U.S.S. *Little Richard*. *Little Richard* was almost three times as big as *Great Christopher* and was the largest warship the world had ever seen. Rumours of her fantastic size had even percolated as far as *Seahorse* and the messes were buzzing with sailors' yarns about her, that she was so big that the Captain went round Sunday divisions in a Grand Prix Ferrari, that her hangars were so large that she carried two squadrons of B.52s, that she was so long that there was a bus service from one end of her to the other, and that her flag deck was so high that her signalmen wore oxygen masks. By any standards she was a formidable ship. The Bodger was anxious to make her acquaintance.

Little Richard was only the hub of a vast armada made up of *Great Christopher* and four smaller carriers, five guided-missile cruisers, three orthodox cruisers, seven escort and radar picket groups, and a fleet train of four tankers and a supply ship.

Occupying last place in the Task Force was the motor yacht *Istagfurallah*, the property of an oil-bearing Sheikh. She was present quite by chance, her owner only hearing of 'Lucky Alphonse' through his sailing master who was given complete details of the exercise in a Naples bar. The Sheikh had arrived at the assembly point first and had courteously greeted each fresh arrival by dipping his ensign, the house flag of San Remo casino, and by a display of fireworks. *Istagfurallah* had passed unchallenged because each new captain who saw her had decided that she must have been included in an Amendment he had not yet received. Her presence was in fact appreciated, if only for the firework display she provided every night. Her only other quirk was her habit of hoisting inexplicable signals according to the passing whim of the Sheikh. At the present moment she was flying 'Am preparing to repel boarders' and a small white pennant inscribed in gold with a verse of the Koran.

By breakfast time, the major units had completed fuelling, the escort groups were in position, and the Task Force moved off on an easterly course, *Istagfurallah* flying the International signal 'You are standing into danger.'

Ten miles ahead, and directly in the path of the Task Force lay S.555, Exercise Callsign: Eskimo Napoleon, H.M.S. *Seahorse* (Lieutenant Commander R. B. Badger, D.S.C., R.N.).

*   *   *

74

Watching the Task Force's advance, The Bodger felt like a bandit waiting to ambush a ponderous wagon train.

'. . . Four, five, *six* escorts. And behind them two carriers. Name of a name. . . . That's the biggest carrier I've ever seen! It's. . . . It's indecent! They're not even zig-zagging. Nearest escort is . . . let's see . . . four miles away. God, talk about Johnny-Head-In-Air! You'd think they were out for a Sunday afternoon jolly. It's always the same with these frigates. Give them a fine afternoon off Portland with the First Eleven up in the Asdic Office and they're good kids. But you wait until they've been at sea a few days and they've had a bit of rough weather and there's any old Joe Bloggs on the set and then you see a difference! They wouldn't know a submarine if it came up and asked them for a light . . .'

'Periscope's been up fifteen seconds, sir,' said Wilfred.

'Right. Let's have another listen.' The Bodger donned the earphones.

By now the attack team had closed up and were waiting for the attack to begin. The control room was crowded with men standing by instruments, plots and counters to help The Bodger with his attack.

'That's a funny H.E.,' The Bodger said.

'I think he's got a chipped propeller, sir,' said Leading Seaman Gorbles. 'I can't get a rev. count on him. He's staggering his revs.'

'Dead crafty,' said The Bodger.

The Bodger took the periscope again.

'Now here's a character who looks as though he knows what he's doing. I do believe it's our friend with the chipped prop. Yes, it must be. Well, here goes. Bring all tubes to the action state. Stand by for the first range and bearing of the target. The target is *Little Richard*. There can't be anyone else that size . . .'

With the first range and bearing of *Little Richard*, the stop watches were started, the first situation put on the fire control plot and the first entry made in the attack narrative. The attack was under way. Meanwhile, The Bodger returned to the ship with the intriguing propellers.

'I don't like the look of this man. He's got the attack flag at the dip. He's got a sniff of us. Ah, he's turned away. His pennant number is F.787. Somebody get out the exercise bridge card and see who that is.'

'It's H.M.S. *Windfall*, sir,' said Wilfred. 'Frigate converted from a destroyer, sir.'

'Who's her captain?'

'Captain J. A. S. Persimmons, D.S.O. and Bar, D.S.C. and Bar, R.N., sir.'

'*Black Sebastian!*'

The Bodger put up the periscope handles with a snap.

'I'd forgotten he was in this exercise!'

The Bodger caught Wilfred's eye.

'*That*,' he said sombrely, 'puts a different complexion on it *altogether*. With Black Sebastian in the hunt this is not going to be as easy as I thought.'

'*Black Sebastian!*'

The control room echoed the words. So might souls abandoned in hell have whispered the syllables of Prince Lucifer's name.

6

Captain Jasper Abercrombie Sebastian Persimmons, D.S.O*., D.S.C*., R.N., known in and out of the submarine service as Black Sebastian, was a living justification of the principle of setting a thief to catch a thief. An ex-submariner himself, he had become the finest anti-submarine captain afloat. His knowledge of submarines and their capabilities and his insight into the mind and thoughts of a submarine captain made him a deadly opponent.

There had often been speculation inside the submarine service on the cause of Black Sebastian's return to general service. The popular theory was that the number of submarine officers Black Sebastian returned to general service through nervous breakdowns became too great a drain on the submarine service's manpower.

Whatever the reason, Black Sebastian now hated submariners with the unreasoning, implacable hatred of a renegade for his former companions. His hatred had made his perceptions keener. Just as Captain Ahab, with almost supernatural accuracy, could foretell the presence of Moby Dick, so Black Sebastian, by nothing more than the pricking of his thumbs, could feel the presence of a submarine. 'I can *see* a periscope at five miles,' he once said, 'and I can *smell* a snort at ten.'

It was no idle boast. Black Sebastian had proved it again and again, flushing a submarine from cover where his rival escort captains had drawn blank. Now, as he swept across the van of the Task Force, Black Sebastian sensed the familiar tingling which told him he was close. Although his asdic operator had only caught a fleeting contact and had been unable to classify it, Black Sebastian knew in his bones that he was getting warm.

Sixty feet down and three miles to starboard, The Bodger was well aware of his danger.

'Sonar, give me constant reports on that H.E. Designate Black Sebastian.'

'Designate Black Sebastian, sir, roger. Black Sebastian, three-five-five, moving rapidly right, transmissions varying.'

The Bodger's attack was already nearing completion. The attack team had re-created from the stream of bearings and ranges The Bodger had given them a plan picture of what The Bodger could see through the periscope. They had also made predictions and deductions which The Bodger could not see and fed them into the calculation. Now, the final firing bearings were approaching solution.

'Black Sebastian fading, zero-zero-five.'

'He'll be back,' said The Bodger. 'Bugger him. Up periscope.'

An attack on a task force through a defending screen was the supreme test of a submarine captain's skill and judgment. It was also a severe strain on his temper. Captains had been known to trample members of their attack teams underfoot and physically to assault their trimming officers if the periscope dipped below the surface for an instant. With such captains, an attack was such excellent entertainment that the sailors who were not in the attack team drew lots for the privilege of standing in the passageway whence they could hear the sound-track.

The Bodger was using the smallest periscope for periods of five seconds, just long enough to take one all-round look and a range and bearing of the target. While the periscope was down, The Bodger paced the control room, crossing from the periscope to the plot, from the plot to the sonar room, and from the sonar room back to the periscope, executing as he went a nervous, jerking hop and jump, like an abbreviated Hungarian mazurka. He wiped the palms of his hands on the seat of his trousers each time before seizing the periscope handles.

'Bodger Agonistes,' murmured Dagwood.

The Bodger was in a perfect attacking position, if the Task Force maintained its present course. He had no need to manœuvre to close the track, nor was there any danger of him being overrun. He was like a swordsman who need do nothing except allow his opponent to run upon his weapon.

'*Surely* they must zig soon. I'm bloody certain Black Sebastian got a sniff of us.'

'Black Sebastian faded. Last bearing zero-two-zero.'

'I wonder what that crafty old bastard's up to now?'

Black Sebastian was huddled on the starboard wing of his bridge, scowling at the sea. He was a very tall man with a hooked nose and a broad black beard. His complexion was pale and his eyes shadowed in deep sockets and he had the pointed ear-tips and arched eyebrows of a Rubens satyr, but his face lacked the same jolly devilment. His whole appearance suggested a powerful

79

but hostile personality. As he leaned over the rail and studied the disposition of the Task Force, he looked like the re-incarnation of a medieval torturer, or one of those terrible figures of the Inquisition who would eat a good dinner and go downstairs to watch their servants with fire and rack extort a recantation.

'We've gone too far.'

Black Sebastian's Navigating Officer was a very brave man, the only man in *Windfall* who dared to question the Captain.

'I think it more likely we'll find him ahead of the Task Force, sir,' he said. 'After all, sir, we're only five miles inside the first submarine area . . .'

'*I tell you we've gone too far you incompetent nincompoop!* He's got past us. We'd better get back there before he does any damage. Starboard thirty . . .'

Windfall and her two wing escorts wheeled back towards the Task Force.

'Five degrees to go, sir!'

The Bodger was nearing his moment of truth. *Little Richard* now filled the whole of the periscope aperture. The Bodger could see every detail of her mammoth sides and superstructure, the aircraft ranged on the flight deck and the men moving around them. The Bodger felt that he only needed to get just a little closer to be able to read the names on the backs of their overalls. Swinging right, The Bodger could see *Windfall's* silhouette lengthening on the horizon as she turned. He's clicked, thought The Bodger, but he's just too damned late.

'On, sir!'

'*Shoot!*'

'Stand by One . . . Fire. Stand by Two . . . Fire.'

Wilfred steadily counted off the torpedoes. The submarine shuddered as they left the tubes. A new sound, an angry buzzing like the whine of a nest of infuriated hornets, invaded Leading Seaman Gorbles' ears.

'Torpedoes running, sir.'

Windfall's asdic operator also picked up the sound and timidly, like a man who knows his voice will release an avalanche, he reported it.

'Torpedo H.E., three-one-five, moving right, sir.'

'*WHAT!*'

Black Sebastian's roar shook the bridge windows. He stood stock-still, his lips trembling, his fingers clenching and unclenching, and for one delirious moment *Windfall's* action bridge team thought their Captain was about to drop dead of a stroke. But they had underestimated their man. Black Sebastian may have been temporarily unbalanced by fury but in the few seconds which had elapsed since he heard the report of the torpedoes he had seen *Little Richard's* emergency turn to comb the torpedo tracks, he had estimated the torpedoes' probable course, and he had already calculated the possible position of the submarine.

'Steer two-six-zero.'

'*Contact*, sir, probable submarine, two-six-five!'

Black Sebastian recovered himself in time to prevent an undignified yell of triumph.

'Now we've got him! Steer two-six-five.' He glowered round his bridge action team. 'If he gets away, I'll break the lot of you,' he said sincerely.

Like many large ladies, U.S.S. *Little Richard* was quick

on her feet. But she was not quick enough. *Seahorse's* six torpedoes, set to run deep, spread out and enveloped her in a wide fan, passing ahead, underneath and close astern of her. The torpedoes were expendable and ran on until their fuel was exhausted and then sank. For exercise purposes, however, they had done their work. *Little Richard* had been sunk, or at best, badly damaged.

The Bodger could not resist remaining at the periscope to witness the results of his handiwork until Leading Seaman Gorbles' voice recalled him to more pressing matters.

'Black Sebastian regained, louder, moving left, zero-four-zero. Transmissions constant, transmission interval four thousand yards. *In contact, sir!*'

'Let's get the hell out of this,' said The Bodger. 'Flood "Q". I think we've overstayed our welcome as it is.'

It would be foolish to stay gloating at the periscope and run into the arms of the escorts, like a man who carried out the perfect bank robbery and was still there admiring his own brilliance when the police arrived.

Just before the periscope dipped, The Bodger caught a glimpse of Black Sebastian and his two henchmen. They made a brave sight, approaching at full speed, their quarterdecks almost submerged in the soaring wakes, their bows flinging spray over the mastheads, and the attack flags whipping at the yard-arms.

'Cor crikey,' said The Bodger admiringly. 'They've got their tails up now and no mistake . . .'

'Black Sebastian zero-three-five, bearing constant, transmissions constant, transmission interval two thousand five hundred yards, *attacking, sir!*'

'Blow "Q" sir?' asked Derek, looking anxiously at his depth gauges, which were unreeling as though demented.

'Not yet. Where's the layer here?'

'Marked one at two hundred and fifty feet, sir,' said Wilfred. 'Slight one at five-fifty.'

'Seven hundred feet,' The Bodger ordered. 'Planes hard a-dive. Lose the bubble, Coxswain.'

Seahorse dropped like a bird with folded wings. No asdic set was needed to hear Black Sebastian now. The ghostly bats' squeaks of his transmissions could be heard plainly against the hull. Black Sebastian was coming down upon them like Sennacherib himself. The Bodger had the eerie sensation that he could feel the man's personality reaching down to grapple him. The Bodger made up his mind.

'Blow "Q." Full ahead together. Hard a starboard!'

Seahorse slipped sideways and downwards in a tight circle which took her underneath the heart of the Task Force where The Bodger stopped the shafts. *Seahorse* glided on under her own momentum, leaving behind her a curling wake of turbulent water which made an excellent asdic target. Black Sebastian's henchmen pounced gleefully upon it and began to weave their complicated ritual patterns above it.

'Black Sebastian very faint, one-seven-eight, no transmissions. Lost contact, sir.'

Now what the hell's he up to? The Bodger asked himself.

'They sought it with thimbles, they sought it with care,' said Dagwood, aloud.

'They threatened its life with a railway share,' continued The Bodger, grinning. 'Fall out the attack team.'

Black Sebastian admitted himself nonplussed. He lashed himself, and his asdic control crew, with his self-reproach. He had committed one of the basic errors of warfare. He had underestimated his opponent. The juicy target upon which he had urged his group had been whipped away and a dummy substituted. Black Sebastian did not believe for a moment that his group were investigating a real contact. He understood very well what the submarine captain had done. It was a manœuvre Black Sebastian had practised many times himself. Furthermore, the submarine captain, whoever he was, had jinked the right way, diving into the middle of the Task Force where Black Sebastian was baulked by the train of surface ships.

Remembering that lightning evasion, Black Sebastian began to wonder about the submarine captain. There were very few submarines in the exercise with such a turn of speed.

'Pilot, get me the bridge exercise card.'

Black Sebastian ran his eye down the list of submarines.

'H.M.S. *Terrapin*, H.M.S. *Angelfish*. *Farfarelli*, the Italian. *La Veuve*, the Frenchman. The Nuclear Job. *Seahorse* . . . *Seahorse*.'

It was too late to chase through the middle of the Task Force now. Black Sebastian decided that it would be better to wait in the rear. Sooner or later, the submarine would come up and then, Black Sebastian thumped a fist into his palm, he would be waiting. Black Sebastian signalled that he had lost contact and withdrew to the rear of the Task Force. He could see an American escort group on the far side taking up the search where he had left off.

'And the best of All-American luck to you too,' growled Black Sebastian.

Between Black Sebastian and the Americans, H.M.S. *Great Christopher* was preparing to launch aircraft.

'*Great Christopher* about to launch aircraft, sir,' said the Navigating Officer.

'I can see that, blast you. If they'd flown off that search at *dawn*, when they bloody well should have done, they would have kept that submarine down until we got past. As it is, against the sort of submarine these vermin are building themselves these days, they're pissing against the wind, that's all they're doing.'

Looking like an Inquisitor faced with a more than usually obstinate heretic, Black Sebastian hunched himself in his bridge chair and settled down to wait.

The Bodger raised his glass.

'Well, men. Here's to Black Sebastian, bless his cotton socks.'

'Cheers, sir,' said the rest of the wardroom. It was very rare for any of the wardroom to drink during an exercise but, as Wilfred said, it was not every day you crashed an escort screen at its strongest point, fired six fish into the largest warship afloat and got clear away again.

'We'll stay here for a couple of hours,' The Bodger said. 'See if the shouting and tumult dies down a bit. Then we'll hop up and make our damage report. I've just realised, we didn't even make an enemy sighting report.'

'I think it's just as well, sir,' said Wilfred. 'That would have given us away before we'd even had a chance to get close.'

'Probably. What course did we estimate the Task Force was steering, Pilot?'

'Due East, sir.'

'Well, we'll steer that for a bit. With any luck we might get another shot!'

'That must have given Black Sebastian something to think about, sir,' said Dagwood. 'I'd love to have seen his face when he realised he'd lost contact.'

The Bodger shook his head. 'We haven't finished with him yet by a long chalk. Black Sebastian isn't the sort of man who gives up as easily as that. You've got to appreciate that he isn't really exercising with you at all. He positively hates you. He wants to see us and all submariners wiped out for good. He looks upon us as vermin, to be stamped out on sight. The most important thing to realise about this whole business is that the best anti-submarine weapon the Navy's ever had and is ever likely to have is the personality of the escort captain. It all comes down to human terms in the long run. I remember a fellow who commanded a frigate during the war telling me that he only actually *saw* a U-boat once, after they'd forced it to the surface in the Atlantic. He said that when he saw that *shape* lying there on the water, he quite literally saw red. His first impulse was to charge down on it and ram it and batter it to death, shoot all the survivors and hang any that he missed from the yard-arm at once. Now, when a man like that manages to control himself and harnesses the energy he generates to a frigate's ship's company, *that's* when people like us have got to look out! Black Sebastian is like that. He's the kind who never gives up. He'll chase up every disappearing radar contact and investigate every echo. He makes everyone's lives a misery to them but he gets results and when he *does* get a submarine . . . He'll stay with it until Doomsday.'

Just before noon, The Bodger yielded to Gavin's suggestion that they go up for a sextant shot of the sun's meridian altitude. *Seahorse* came up to a hundred feet while Leading Seaman Gorblés listened carefully all round for any sign of hydrophone effect. Hearing nothing, *Seahorse* rose cautiously to periscope depth. The Bodger had no sooner taken his first look through the periscope

86

when he flooded 'Q' and ordered a depth of seven hundred feet again.

'Jesus!' he said. 'It was some kind of bloody yacht, stopped about twenty yards away! It was so damned close that all I could see through the periscope at first was a row of bloody rivets!'

At noon, Black Sebastian got up from his chair and stretched. If he was a submarine captain, he would be coming up just about now.

'Old *Istagfurallah* is very excited about something, sir,' said the Navigating Officer.

'What's that?'

'He seems to've got some bee in his burnous . . .'

Black Sebastian snatched up his binoculars. *Istagfurallah* was steaming excitedly round in small circles, firing off salvoes of fireworks and sounding long blasts on her siren.

'I'll tell you what he's got, you cretin!' bellowed Black Sebastian. 'He's got a submarine! While we sit here in several million quids' worth of frigate with our thumbs in our bums a flea-ridden Sheikh squatting on his prayer-mat does everything but gaff our target for us! Look at them!' Black Sebastian gestured at his wing escorts, nosing industriously about on each side. 'Bloody square-eyed addicts with free-flood ears, goggling all day long into their infernal idiots' lanterns and flapping their ears at a lot of clicks and bangs! They should get out into the fresh air for once where they can see what's happening! My God, we're going to be too late *again!*'

The spectacle of Black Sebastian and his two henchmen closing him at maximum speed was too much for the Sheikh. It had been a disturbing morning all round. First, an infidel periscope had broken the sacred hour of noon and nothing discommoded a true believer more than being spied on by strangers at his devotions. Now he was menaced by three Touareg frigates, the Forgotten of God. It was too much. The Sheikh swung round and withdrew to the south. Flying a banner which read: 'Go Home Lawrence' the Sheikh disappeared rapidly over the horizon and took no further part in the exercise.

'*Now* we'll get him!' cried Black Sebastian. The Sheikh had given them an excellent datum position.

But The Bodger was not to be caught a second time. He went deep, lay very low, and like Brer Rabbit, said nothing. Black Sebastian searched vainly for six hours and then withdrew under instructions from the flag-ship. When The Bodger returned to periscope depth in the late evening, he found a clear sea and sky.

There were also three signals. Two concerned a gauge for the distiller and The Bodger threw them away without letting the details register on his mind.

'Here am I,' he said, 'trying to put one over the best anti-submarine captain in the service and they send me signals about distillers.'

The third signal, however, caused The Bodger's eyebrows to shoot up. The suddenness and brilliance of The Bodger's attack on *Little Richard* had thrown the planning staff ashore into some understandable confusion (mixed with resentment that The Bodger had presumed to create an incident while they were still setting up the counters on the plotting floor). The third signal was from Com-SubPink and read: 'Proceed at best speed.'

The Bodger thought for a moment, replied: 'Where?', and set *Seahorse* snorting at maximum speed to the eastwards.

In two hours the answer returned from ComSubPink: 'Exercise Area Banana.'

The Bodger stroked his chin and came back with a shrewd thrust: 'Am in Exercise Area Banana.'

'I can almost hear the wheels turning,' The Bodger said, as he turned into his bunk.

At midnight, the Petty Officer Telegraphist decoded the top secret priority signal: 'Remain on patrol in Exercise Area Banana.'

'Ah . . . *splendid* exercise,' said The Bodger.

At one o'clock in the morning a Coastal Command aircraft returning off task over the Bay of Biscay picked up a small intermittent radar contact. The contact was at extreme range and the aircraft did not have sufficient fuel to make a proper investigation. It was hardly enough evidence on which to begin a submarine hunt. But it was more than enough for Black Sebastian.

7

At half-past two Black Sebastian was shaken by the bridge messenger.

'From the Officer of the Watch, we're at the position now, sir.'

'Very good.'

Still fully dressed, Black Sebastian swung out of his bunk and went out on to the bridge.

'We're at the aircraft datum position, sir,' said the Navigating Officer.

'I know,' said Black Sebastian brusquely. He crossed to the wing of the bridge. It was a very dark close night. The stars were obscured by a low ceiling of cloud. Below him Black Sebastian could just make out great white lines of foam racing out to *Voluminous* who was keeping station three cables away on the starboard beam. All ships were darkened. Or supposed to be darkened.

'Make to *Voluminous*: You have a bright light showing from your sea cabin.'

'Aye aye, sir.'

Black Sebastian came back into the compass platform.

'He's not here,' he said. 'If I was him I would be going like a bat out of hell. We won't find him just yet. How many look-outs have you got, Officer of the Watch?'

'Two, sir.'

'Double them. How long has the radar watchkeeper been on watch?'

'An hour and three-quarters, sir.'

'Have him relieved. And relieve the sonar watchkeeper as well. I want everyone fresh. We can expect him any time from now on and I expect he's pretty tired by now.'

Black Sebastian knew from his own experience the effect on a submarine ship's company of snorting at top speed for most of the night. If there was any time for catching a submarine napping, it was between two and three o'clock in the morning.

'I bet there's not a man on watch in that submarine who hasn't got his eye firmly fixed on the clock. Make to *Voluminous* and *Octopus*: Cease operating radar. Switch on navigation lights. Keep radio and sonar silence.'

The three ships were already steaming too fast for their asdic sets to be of much use but Black Sebastian had a poor idea of the mental capabilities of his fellow captains.

'I wouldn't put it past them to go spoiling everything with their eager beaver transmissions. They've been reading too many text-books and listening to too many lectures. Come down to twelve knots. I want to have a listen.'

The escort group had barely eased to twelve knots and the fresh asdic operator had hardly taken his seat when Black Sebastian's heart was made glad within him.

'Steady H.E., one-one-zero, sir.'

Black Sebastian steadied his voice.

'Classify.'

'Possible submarine diesel, sir. Too fast for a rev. count, sir.'

'Let me hear.'

Black Sebastian listened to the steady, unmistakable rumbling and let out a sigh.

'That's him . . .'

'From *Voluminous* and *Octopus*, sir, Have contact, classified snorting submarine.'

'Acknowledge. Now we'll just follow.' Black Sebastian rubbed his hands. 'Until the water gets nice and shallow . . .'

Black Sebastian had described the position in *Seahorse* exactly. Rusty and Dagwood were on watch and heartily tired of it. Rusty was on the periscope and Dagwood was marking the plot and both were longing for the next forty minutes to pass when they would be relieved by Wilfred and the Midshipman.

'Any sign of that light-house yet, Rusty?'

'Not a thing. Nothing but those three merchantmen. Wait a minute, that might have been the loom of a light just now. Trouble is that it's so bloody dark that half the time I don't know whether I'm looking at the horizon or not. I have to keep coming back to those merchantmen to fix myself. We'll have to tell the Boss about them soon, Dagwood. They're getting quite close. Yes . . . There it is again!'

Rusty stared at the loom of the light. It was less of a loom than a slight lifting of the darkness on the horizon.

'Yes, that's it definitely. Half a minute while I try and get the time. Group flashing four every fifteen, or thereabouts. How about that?'

'Sounds like it. I'll tell the Boss.'

The Bodger came awake as the first footstep touched the sill of his cabin door. The long days with little sleep had fined down his perceptions; he awoke now to the sound of an eyelash fluttering.

'What bearing is it?'

'Zero-seven-six, sir.'

'Good. We must have made better time than I thought. The tide must be with us. Anything else in sight?'

'Only three merchantmen, sir.'

'*What three merchantmen?*'

'About five miles astern, sir . . .'

The Bodger sprang from his bunk as though galvanised by a sudden tremendous current. He thrust Rusty away from the periscope, looked in it for a moment, and then raced to the sonar room. The watchkeeper, a somnolent rating named Perkins, snapped rigid in his seat at the sight of the Captain and began to operate his set industriously. The Bodger seized a pair of earphones and listened intently.

'Stop snorting! Action stations! Attack team close up!' The Bodger turned on Rusty and Dagwood. 'Do you know what you've done, you cloth-eared clowns? You've delivered us up into the hands of the Anti-Christ!'

'H.E. faded, sir.'

Black Sebastian's face creased in an executioner's smile.

'Hah, they've woken up at last. Action stations. We'll get him now, once and for all.'

Rubbing the sleep from their eyes, *Seahorse's* ship's company dragged themselves to their action stations. The Bodger stood at the periscope scourging them into their places with his tongue. Leading Seaman Gorbles' voice took over on the sonar broadcast; there was no need to tell him where the greatest danger lay.

'Black Sebastian two-eight-three moving right transmissions . . . on the bearing . . .'

Leading Seaman Gorbles' sleep-drugged brain translated the information passed to him by the sonar automatically. His training had been so drilled into him that he could have passed sonar bearing changes while in a hypnotic trance.

It was almost too late for The Bodger to evade Black Sebastian, but not quite.

'Black Sebastian moving right two-eight-seven . . .'

The Bodger had one last manoeuvre up his sleeve. 'Port thirty. Steer two-nine-zero.'.

'. . . Transmissions constant, *attacking, sir.*'

'Full ahead together!'

'. . . Two-eight-eight . . .'

'What's *Windfall's* keel depth, somebody?'

'Seventeen feet, sir,' said Wilfred.

The Bodger made a rapid addition of *Windfall's* keel depth and the height of his own fin.

'Keep eighty feet.'

As *Windfall* closed on her final attacking course, *Seahorse* darted towards her at full speed, passed directly underneath her, swayed in her wake while the noise of her passage clamoured against the pressure hull, and slid astern of her.

'. . . Black Sebastian all round H.E. *very loud* . . .'

The Bodger guessed that Black Sebastian would probably turn to port and turned to port also. He could not go deep. They were now less than fifteen miles from land and the water was already beginning to shallow.

'Unless we're bloody careful,' The Bodger announced

94

to the control room at large, 'Black Sebastian's going to land us high and dry. What's the tide doing, Pilot?'

'Setting round the point, sir,' said Gavin. 'Quite strongly too, sir.'

'We'll stay doggo and let the tide carry us quietly away.'

'But oh, beamish nephew, beware of the day,' said Dagwood to himself, 'if your Snark be a Boojum. For then you will softly . . . and silently . . . vanish away.'

Dagwood sighed. It was not nearly so funny at three o'clock in the morning.

'Lost contact, sir.'

'Yes, I thought you had,' Black Sebastian said bitterly.

Once again, he pondered on the nature of his enemy. These bursts of speed could only be done by a handful of boats in the exercise. That narrowed the field. But the last burst, right under the attacking frigate, narrowed the field still more; it could only have been done by a certain type of captain. Black Sebastian had felt the submarine pass underneath him, through the very soles of his feet, and he had to admit himself taken aback. It had been such a flamboyant, theatrical gesture; one might have expected it from Metro-Goldwyn-Mayer, but not from a modern submarine captain. Black Sebastian studied the bridge card again. Once more, *Seahorse* caught his eye.

'Badger.' Black Sebastian pursed his lips. 'Badger. Never heard of him.'

Black Sebastian's memory could not recall a young sub-lieutenant who had joined Black Sebastian's submarine straight from his training class and who had refused to be crushed by his captain's personality.

'What's the tide doing, Pilot?'

95

'Setting strongly to the north, sir.'

'He's bound to be carried by the tide whether he likes it or not. So we'll drive him. Between the tide and the land and the three of us, we should get him eventually. Operate radar.'

'We should be getting up to the twenty fathom line any time now, sir,' Gavin said.

'That's all right,' said The Bodger. 'We're allowed to go over it in this exercise. We're supposed to act as in war. And with Black Sebastian breathing down your neck, it is. Keep sixty feet.'

Seahorse planed upwards.

'What time does it get light?'

'Just before six o'clock, sir,' said Wilfred.

'Another two and a half hours of darkness. I hope that will be enough. Up periscope. What's this? Looks like a fishing fleet. How's your French, Dagwood?'

'Not too bad, sir.'

'We'll be needing it. Right, Number One, I want to do an old-fashioned gun action surface. I want to get up there, but quick. I want a single white light to go on top of the fin. And a whistle. Have you got a whistle?'

'I can get one, sir,' said Wilfred.

'Get it. Rusty, you'll surface the boat. Have you ever done a gun action surface?'

'No, sir.'

'All you've got to do is let go the upper lid when I blow the whistle. Now let's have a pressure in the boat. Open "Q" inboard vent and blow "Q".'

'Open "Q" inboard vent and blow "Q", sir,' said the Outside Wrecker, who knew exactly what to do. This was quite like old times.

Air poured into 'Q' tank and out through the open vent into the submarine until the barometers showed an excess pressure of more than two inches.

'That's enough. Let's have a sailor with the light following up the Torpedo Officer.'

'Here's the whistle, sir. It belongs to the ship's football team.'

'Splendid! Ready?'

'Yes, sir. Ready to surface.'

'Stand by to surface, full ahead together, planes hard a dive! *Dive* man,' said The Bodger to the Coxswain, who was looking round incredulously.

Seahorse began to sink.

'Blow all main ballast!'

Air pressing into the tanks slowly counteracted the effect of the hydroplanes. *Seahorse* stopped sinking and began to rise.

'Planes hard a rise! Switch on navigation lights.'

Under the combined effect of hydroplanes and the main ballast tanks, *Seahorse* rose like a cork. While the upper hatch was still under water, The Bodger blew the whistle. Rusty let go the hatch and rose up with the rush of escaping air. A spectator would have thought that *Seahorse* had surfaced with Rusty already on deck.

'Chop chop with that light!'

The single light was rigged and switched on. The bow lights were already burning. From a distance, *Seahorse* quickly became indistinguishable from the mass of fishing vessels pressing all around her.

'Still no contact, sir.'

'I don't believe it! She *must* be there! There's nowhere else she could have gone!'

97

'She might be among all those fishing vessels, sir,' ventured the Navigating Officer.

'When I want your advice I'll ask for it!' Black Sebastian crossed to the radar screen. 'Radar, did you count the echoes of that fishing fleet?'

'No, sir?'

'Well, why the devil not?'

'But sir, there's *dozens* of them, sir! I'd be all *night* counting them, sir!'

The radar operator's voice faltered when he discovered the Captain was actually looking over his shoulder. The Captain's voice sent chilly shivers up and down the radar operator's backbone.

'Now look here. When I tell you to count radar echoes, you count radar echoes. I want to know if an extra one appears or one of them disappears.'

'Ay-aye aye, sir.'

'We seem to be attracting quite a bit of attention, sir,' said Dagwood.

Voluble Gallic cries of alarm were coming out of the night.

'So we are,' said The Bodger. 'What're they saying?'

'They want to know who we are, sir.'

'Quite right, too. Tell them we're the Mademoiselle de Paris, two days out of Montmartre.'

Dagwood translated to the nearest fishing vessel. More vehement shouts sailed out of the dark.

'I don't think that was the right thing to say, sir.'

'Why not?'

'They seem to think we're a Russian submarine, sir.'

'Good God, that's the unkindest cut of all! You'd better tell them who we really are. And tell them those ships out there are really the Russians. Who's the Officer of the Watch now?'

'I am, sir,' said Wilfred.

'I want to stay up here as long as it's dark. Keep in the middle of this fishing fleet but try not to hit any nets or anything. You'd better try and smell of garlic and fish, too. Have you got a beret?'

'I'm afraid not, sir.'

'Pity. You'll just have to hum a few snatches of the "Marseillaise" now and then. Let me know if Black Sebastian comes too close or if he looks as though he's got us. Dagwood, have you got your tape-recorder handy?'

'It's in the wardroom, sir.'

'You'd better get it warmed up. I want to use it.'

Seahorse remained inside the fishing fleet (contrary to Admiralty Instructions, but The Bodger was a desperate man) until dawn and then dived. Black Sebastian and his two henchmen probed cautiously along the fringes of the fishing fleet but their radar was defeated by the multitude of echoes and their sonar listening was confused by the water disturbances under the fishing fleet. The two henchmen moved out to seaward, pinging disconsolately as they went. Black Sebastian stayed with the fishing fleet, like a terrier refusing to leave a rat-hole. Just after dawn he was rewarded by a contact.

'Underwater telephone, sir.'

Black Sebastian lifted a weary head. 'Put it over the bridge broadcast.'

There came a hollow roaring, as though Neptune himself were clearing his throat, and then unmistakably the throbbing of drums, the wailing of a clarinet and the cheeky metallic voice of a calypso steel band singer.

'*Where* did the naughty little flea go? Nobody know, nobody know!'

99

Black Sebastian glanced round his bridge team. They were all poised, ready to start the attack again.

'Where did the naughty little *flea* go? *Nobody* know nobody know!'

The bridge action team tensed.

'Where did the *naughty* little flea go? *Nobody* know nobody know!'

'Switch that thing off,' said Black Sebastian. 'Pilot, give me a course to rejoin the Task Force.'

At breakfast time, The Bodger sat down to as fine a grilled sole as he had ever set eyes on. Two bottles of whisky had procured fish for breakfast, lobster for supper, and three bottles of a violent purple vin ordinaire.

'I'm very grateful to Black Sebastian,' The Bodger said. 'If it hadn't been for him we'd be sitting down to the same old bangers and train smash. It's almost worthwhile meeting him again.'

But they did not meet Black Sebastian again. They did not in fact meet anyone again. One day they saw an aircraft pass low on the horizon and on another day they investigated a target which proved to be a whale factory ship, but the main battle had passed them by. From time to time they intercepted signals which plotted the path of the Task Force eastwards and northwards as the submarines, one by one, rose to attack it like dogs leaping at a bear. The rest of the time they spent waiting for the signal which would release them.

As soon as the magic signal was received, submarines popped to the surface all over the Western Approaches and set off determinedly towards hot baths, liquor and women. Most of them arrived together and the water around Spithead was soon churned into a foam by submarines of various nationalities queueing up to enter the channel, getting in each other's way and sending each other fatuous signals.

Seahorse joined the queue with her control room watch singing their home-coming song: 'First the Nab and then the Warner, Outer Spit and Blockhouse Corner' led with great feeling by Able Seaman Geronwyn Evans, to the tune of Cwm Rhondda.

When The Bodger saw the milling throng of submarines he felt that he was among friends again. He had had a good exercise, for a new boy (The Bodger was sure that even his most jealous critics in the Staff Office would admit that) and it was good to be home again. The Bodger's heart swelled. He wanted to be hospitable.

'When's the Wash-Up?'

'Tuesday, sir,' said Wilfred.

'Tell the wireless office to make to all submarines in company: R.P.C. *Seahorse*, 1900, Monday. We'll have a Wake. If we're going to tell lies we might as well all tell the same one. Who's that just ahead of us?'

'*Terrapin*, sir,' said Wilfred.

'Who's driving her now?'

'Lieutenant Commander Lamm, sir.'

Lieutenant Commander Lamm was one of the keenest captains in the submarine service, so much so that he was known as the Lamm of God. He had reasonably expected to be given the command of *Seahorse* himself.

'Make to *Terrapin*. You're a Blue submarine, I'm a Pink submarine, do we both use the same toothpaste?'

The Bodger was enormously amused by his own joke. Looking at him, Dagwood was reminded of a schoolboy coming home for the holidays.

Meanwhile, the Signalman was occupied with his lamp.

'From *Terrapin*, sir,' he said. 'Negative. Pepsodent.'

The Bodger groaned. 'My God, what can you do with a bloke like that? Ask him where the yellow went. . . . No, no forget it. *Now*, what have we here?'

The last addition to the queue was a huge steel-grey vessel with blunt bows and a swollen body. The short Channel waves were sweeping over her casing. She was as plainly out of her element as a whale in a backwater stream.

'There,' said The Bodger, 'goes the future. Actually, it's the present now. This mighty vessel of ours is the biggest, fastest and most dangerous submarine we've got but compared with that ugly-looking lump over there we're about as lethal as a baby's bottle!' The Bodger put up his binoculars. 'That monstrosity is the biggest technical break-through since . . . since the discovery of the wheel. She can stay at sea as long as Moby Dick, she's faster than a destroyer and she's got a weapon that can blast across the Arctic circle and blot out a whole city. They've pinched a bit of fire from the sun and put it inside that submarine.'

'Cor chase me old Aunt Fanny round the dockyard clock,' said the Signalman to himself, 'the Captain's a bloody poet!'

'Stop *muttering*, Signalman!' said The Bodger.

8

Exercise 'Lucky Alphonse' had been important enough—
in its own way. It had provided a great many people
with harmless employment and with justification for
their existences. As Exercises went, it had been a fair
success. But 'Lucky Alphonse' was only a prelude and
insignificant beside its aftermath, the Post-Exercise
Analytical Discussion, known colloquially as The
Wash-Up.

'Lucky Alphonse' had been a mock battle. The Wash-
Up was a real and bitter struggle. It was the battle-
ground of the Staff, the faceless officers who stood behind
the Admirals, the authors of the indecipherable signatures
on the minute sheets. The Wash-Up was not concerned
with the security of nations, nor the exchange of tactical
information nor the learning of lessons taught at sea but
with the more urgent and personal matters of furthering
reputations and consummating careers. Those officers
who would have agitated for commands in wartime, in
peacetime angled for staff appointments. Command in
peacetime was too often the prelude to retirement. It was
not fashionable to step on to one's own bridge and take
command of events. It was more profitable to stay ashore
and create the events. A successful exercise was therefore

not one which tested the defences of the nation at sea but one after which the entire staff were promoted.

There were no Orders for the Wash-Up. Only sham battles needed Orders. Real battles took their cue from a hint, from a judiciously-timed signal, from a face-saving suggestion or a tiny oversight in the opposition planning. The real battles did not take place in the sonar and radar control rooms but in the signal centres and the plotting floors. The sounds of victory were not uttered by gunfire but by the clatter of cryptographic machinery.

The Bodger took Wash-Ups, like everything else, in his stride.

'They're all the same,' he said to Gavin, who was hard at work preparing *Seahorse's* track charts and attack narratives. 'You never get a word in edgeways anyway. The R.A.F. will be there in force. I sometimes wonder if the R.A.F. don't keep a special Wash-Up *Regiment*. You never see them any other time. The Staff will be there, of course, unto the seventh generation. You can always tell them by their brief-cases and the Japanese binoculars slung round their necks. They're the chappies who always know everything. They tell you all about radio reception conditions over the South Pole and what the correct recognition procedure is when you're challenged by an Abyssinian flying-boat dropping shark repellent but they never tell you anything you really want to *know*, like who that dangerous lunatic was who nearly ran you down the second night out. Then there will be a few blokes like you and me who actually *did* the exercise, and a little man at the back who's waiting to straighten the chairs and empty the ashtrays and get back home to his football pools. And that's about all.'

The Wash-Up was held at nine a.m. in the Royal Naval Barracks cinema, the duty R.P.O. having first ejected a class of Upper Yardmen who had been waiting since a quarter to eight to see an instructional film entitled 'The Ammeter'. The first arrivals were two staff captains of the Indonesian Tank Corps and the last were the Commander-in-Chief, Rockall and Malin Approaches and his staff who included a bewildered young man in a white coat with blue cuffs who had driven a van full of mineral-water bottles up to the Barracks wardroom and had been directed by the hall porter to the cinema along with everybody else.

By nine o'clock the meeting had taken shape. The first three rows bristled with the intelligent faces, clean collars, brief-cases, Japanese binoculars and aiguillettes of the Staff; they formed a barrier of erudition, culture and enthusiasm which it would be difficult to pierce. There was among their ranks much nodding, winking, and secret signs of conspiracy; they were the Magicians who sat pulling strings while their own Petroushkas capered about on the stage.

The next seventeen rows were occupied by R.A.F. officers. They were all moustached, all serious of face, and all holding a sheaf of papers. Behind them sat the hard core of the conference, the captains of *Little Richard*, *Great Christopher* and the guided-missile cruisers, Black Sebastian and the other escort captains, the Master of the fleet tanker *Wave Chiropodist* and several rows of ship's officers who, through many sleepless nights, had made the Exercise work.

In the very back row, in an aura of alcohol, sat the submarine captains and their officers. The Bodger's Pre-Wash-Up Wake had been a spectacular success. At midnight, the captain of the Italian submarine *Farfarelli* had executed a variant of the Limbo Dance which had fetched him up under the wardroom table where he lay babbling faintly of the waters of the Po; he was now leaning back in his seat staring at the ceiling, his face drawn in a mask of torment similar to that of Count Ugolino, who was trapped in the lake of eternal ice and condemned to gnaw upon the skull of his murderer for ever. At two o'clock in the morning, two very correctly dressed officers from the biggest technical break-through since the wheel had called on *Seahorse* to collect their captain, whom they knew affectionately as Ole Miss, who had by that time gone critical. Ole Miss was now sitting propped up at the arm-pits by his Navigating Officer and his Exec, beaming round him with a genial, if slightly vacant, smile. At three o'clock in the morning, the Lamm of God had politely taken his leave, steered himself towards his cabin, and solemnly shut himself in the wardrobe where he spent the rest of the night; he was now sitting bolt upright at one end of the row, looking carefully to his front as though he were afraid that any sudden movement would topple his head from his shoulders. The Bodger himself was flanked by Wilfred, Gavin and Dagwood, all four concentrating on preventing their eyelids meeting.

The proceedings were opened by the Commander-in-Chief, Rockall and Malin Approaches, under his abbreviated international title of CincRock, in whose domain a great part of the Exercise had taken place.

CincRock hated international maritime exercises and in particular he hated 'Lucky Alphonse' because he had been unable to go to sea for a single day of it. He had, in his own words, been 'stuck in a damned beer-cellar gawking at a bloody stupid Monopoly board.' CincRock was a plain seaman who had had greatness thrust upon him. He had served almost continuously at sea until he was promoted to Captain when the shortage of ships forced him for the first time in his life into the Admiralty. There, he was an innocent set adrift in a paper jungle and his immediate impulse had been to retire from the Service. But CincRock possessed one of the most priceless assets of a successful naval officer; he was adaptable. In a paper jungle, he became the most ferocious paper tiger of them all. His other qualities, of remembering what was said last week without looking at the minutes, of dealing with papers within twenty-four hours of receipt, and of catching up with the latest scandal in the pubs of Whitehall, made him tolerated, respected, and then feared. The men who sat at desks and administered the Navy began to speak of him with awe, as a naval officer who had civilised the civil servants.

Nobody suspected that CincRock paid only lip service to Whitehall. None of the men who gazed so benignly at him over their committee tables were aware that Cinc-Rock was their implacable enemy. It was CincRock who was responsible for the closure of the forty-one stores depots scattered through the United Kingdom which had long since ceased to issue stores and were quietly administering themselves. It was CincRock who obtained a new class of ship for the Navy by unobtrusively crossing out the title 'Cruiser' and substituting 'Destroyer' as the relevant correspondence passed through his office (the Treasury subsequently decided that the country could afford a new class of destroyers but not cruisers).

More than anything about 'Lucky Alphonse,' Cinc-Rock hated having to make the speech of welcome at the beginning of the Wash-Up. As he said to his Chief of Staff, 'I feel like a damned chairman congratulating his damned shareholders on how many damned washing machines he's sold for them.'

'My first, and my most pleasant, duty,' said CincRock

at the Wash-Up, 'is to welcome you all here and to congratulate you on your excellent showing during "Lucky Alphonse." This year's exercise was more successful than any we've had in previous years. More nations contributed ships. There were more incidents. And the whole thing went with a bang! One or two things cropped up, particularly on the anti-submarine side, which were not quite as successful as we had hoped for. Submarines made a total of ninety-four attacks. Seventy-nine of those were judged successful. That's a very high percentage. Too high. At the same time, only five submarines were judged sunk, one by aircraft and four by surface ships. That was not so good. My Chief of Staff will deal with that in detail in a few moments. My job now is to say how glad I am to see you all here and to hope you have a damned good time while you're here.'

CincRock nodded to his Chief of Staff who had been standing, a Svengali-like figure, in the background.

The Chief of Staff made an immediate impression upon Dagwood.

'Augustus was a chubby lad,' recited Dagwood irreverently. 'Fat chubby cheeks Augustus had. He ate and drank as he was told, and never let his soup get cold.'

Augustus was a brilliant officer who had risen to the rank of Rear Admiral on a series of staff appointments. As Staff Commander, Staff Captain, and finally as Chief of Staff he had been the eminence grise behind a number of successful admirals, of whom CincRock was the latest. Analytical discussions were Augustus' forte. He was a master strategist, in terms of counters and symbols, a blackboard Bismarck, a veritable Wellington of the Wash-Ups.

'All yours, Gussie,' said CincRock.

Augustus unrolled a map, took up a pointer and began to summarise Exercise 'Lucky Alphonse.' He described the rapid mobilisation which had followed the proclamation of a state of emergency in Western Europe. He outlined the balance of power and the disposition of forces available at the moment the conflict began. He explained the solution of the logistical problems which had made possible the assembly of a vast Task Force of different nations far out in the Atlantic. He traced the progress of the Task Force towards the continent of Europe. Augustus had all the data at his finger-tips. Incidents, times, courses and speeds rolled from his memory. As he expounded, with cross-reference and flash-back, the unfolding of the master exercise plan, every officer present began to understand where his own limited and seemingly unconnected contribution had fitted into the whole. Augustus was like a skilled advocate building, piece by piece, a complicated case in company law and by the time he had completed his summary it was easy to see why he had become a Rear Admiral. His had been the performance of a virtuoso and there was a moment's silence after he had finished speaking, like the momentary hush which precedes the tumultuous applause after a superlative interpretation of a concerto. Indeed, one or two of the more susceptible officers present wondered whether a round of applause might not be in order.

'Well done, Gussie,' said CincRock, *sotto voce*.

The audience were given no more time to decide whether or not Augustus should be given a clap. Augustus had hardly put down his pointer when a Squadron Leader with shiny black hair and a toothbrush moustache had stood up and begun to read rapidly from a sheet of paper.

'At fourteen hundred hours on the ninth, Yoke Uncle was on task over the Bay of Biscay. There was seven-eighths cloud at five thousand feet and a force two breeze from the south-west. Some difficulty was experienced in maintaining radio contact with . . .'

Augustus, who had been about to sign off with a neatly turned phrase which would have thrown the meeting open, remained on the platform, his pointer still poised. He opened and shut his mouth several times without achieving a break-through. The Air Show was exactly timed. Yoke Uncle had hardly landed when Mike Zebra was in the air, piloted by a Flight Lieutenant with a ginger bat-handle moustache. Mike Zebra had maintained radio contact successfully but had had other troubles; her starboard wheel had been reluctant to come up and once up, had refused to go down again. Mike Zebra had barely come to rest in a field by the side of the runway when Delta Eskimo, represented by a Squadron Leader in a bushy black moustache, was airborne and suffering damage to her tail-plane. Fox Pepper, with a reduced Salvador Dali and sad spaniel eyes, had been lost in fog. Indian Queen had not taken off at all. ('The ashtrays were full,' Black Sebastian said in a resonant stage-whisper.) When at last the Air Show ended the admirals and captains of the greatest Grand Alliance in history had been given a thorough exposition of the trials and hardships attached to anti-submarine flying.

CincRock found his voice. 'Did you find any submarines?'

Every flying eye turned towards a pale youth with a faint blond moustache sitting in the back row of the pilots. He was the only pilot who had not yet spoken. The others looked towards him as though to one who had searched for, and found, the Holy Grail. He was their champion, the gentle knight without a blemish. He had seen a submarine.

The gentle knight rose reluctantly to his feet. 'Well, actually, the whole thing was rather a bit of joss,' he said diffidently. 'We were just as surprised to see him as he was to see us. It was very early in the morning. We came suddenly through thick cloud down to about five hundred feet and there he was, lying on the surface. He dived straight away, of course, but we tracked him with sono-buoys until some frigates came up and took over. I believe they got him.'

The gentle knight sat thankfully down again, like Sir Galahad after a press conference.

'Well done,' CincRock said warmly.

After the Air Show there was some general discussion amongst the Task Force and escort captains about tactics. Of the four submarines judged sunk by surface ships, three were credited to Black Sebastian and the fourth to the Captain who had consulted the Second Book of Kings and Hymns Ancient & Modern.

'I nearly got another,' said Black Sebastian, looking balefully at the back row where The Bodger had fallen into a light sleep. 'With one more escort in the right place we'd have got him.'

This remark touched the Wash-Up audience on its most sensitive spot. The shortage of escorts had hampered everyone. The cry was taken up on all sides. Carrier captains complained of being asked to fly off strikes whilst completely unprotected against submarine attack. The Master of *Wave Chiropodist* complained of being detached from the main body to carry out his own anti-submarine search. 'Let me say now, once and for all,' he said, 'no fleet tanker I ever heard of is equipped to look for submarines. I only hope the Unions don't get to hear of it.'

One of the guided missile cruiser captains claimed that he personally had made more submarine detections than either of his two escorts. The escort captains retorted that no anti-submarine vessel yet designed could have covered effectively the areas they had been called upon to patrol. The R.A.F. listened curiously, as deep thus called out deep.

The mineral-water bottle vanman had been sitting in enthralled silence. He had followed every word of Augustus' narrative. The Air Show had been meat and drink to him. He had developed a very high respect for Black Sebastian. But now, as the argument gained momentum, the young man in the blue cuffs began to grow impatient. He fully appreciated that he was probably the most junior person present and was not likely to be called upon for an opinion but he could not allow this discussion to pass without putting forward an obvious solution. It was not in his nature to remain silent when the simplest way to solve the argument must surely be staring everybody in the face.

'Why not build more ships, sir?' he called out.

It was the compelling voice of innocence, the voice of the child who pointed out that the Emperor had no clothes on. It cut through the heated atmosphere of the Wash-Up like a cold fresh wind. The escort captain who had been speaking stopped, frowned, and sat down at once. CincRock stood up and searched the rows of faces.

'Who said that?'

The vanman had been dumbfounded by the effect of his remark. He felt like a small boy who, having mischievously pulled at a small insignificant length of chain, discovers that he has stopped the express.

'Me, sir,' said the vanman, blushing bashfully.

'Well done,' said CincRock. 'That's the first sensible thing I've heard today.'

Staff Officers who had been bursting to deliver themselves of brilliant logistical suggestions changed their minds and decided to put their ideas on paper. Captains who had been reserving their most telling arguments until last decided that perhaps there was nothing further to add after all. The vanman had killed the Wash-Up stone dead.

Just as he was about to close the meeting, CincRock remembered that there was still one community who had not yet made any contribution to the Wash-Up.

'How about the submariners? Anyone want to say anything back there?'

Like the Traveller, knocking on the moonlit door and asking 'Is there anybody there?' CincRock repeated his question.

Dagwood tactfully nudged The Bodger who came awake immediately, stood up and said: 'From our point of view it was a *splendid* exercise! It was a good clean fight, no holds barred, and may the best man win!'

So saying, The Bodger relapsed enigmatically into his seat. His place was taken by Ole Miss who was jerked to his feet by a firm hand under each arm-pit. He was a very short man and he was temporarily suspended, his feet pedalling at the floor, like a gnome on gimbals.

'As a career-motivated officer,' Ole Miss said, 'I can tell you all that Exercise Lucky Alphonse was the goddamned best exercise, logistics-wise and sea-familiarisation-wise, we've ever partakelised. The only time we hit trouble was some goddamned *yacht*. He really scared the juice out of me. . . .!'

Ole Miss stopped, blinked, appeared to have lost the thread of what he was about to say, and was rapidly lowered out of sight.

The only other submarine contribution was from Count Ugolino who shook off his former mask-like torpor and launched a torrent of Italian, embellished with histrionic gestures, flashing eyes and snapping fingers.

The Bodger stirred uneasily. 'Who's that *noisy* bastard?' he enquired irritably. The message was passed along the row to *Farfarelli's* Navigating Officer who spoke softly to his captain. Count Ugolino finished his sentence, bowed low, blew a kiss to CincRock and sat down.

After the Wash-Up CincRock released the normal statement to the press, confirming that 'Lucky Alphonse' had been a complete success, having consolidated the maritime defences of Europe and strengthened once more the bonds which united the nations of the free world.

The only flaw in the confident façade was disclosed by CincRock himself. He was button-holed about 'Lucky Alphonse' by the Naval Correspondent of the *Daily Disaster* outside the 'Keppel's Head' and replied that in his opinion the United Kingdom was no better fitted to defeat a determined submarine attack than it was equipped to beat off a swarm of locusts.

'At least,' CincRock shouted, as he was hustled into his car by his Flag Lieutenant and Augustus, 'we could *eat* the bloody locusts!'

9

'This week,' said The Bodger, 'we really *must* get organised. *Work Study* is the latest cry in the Staff Office at the moment. Apparently we've been doing it all wrong all these years. It seems that what was good enough for Nelson is *not* good enough for us after all. Everybody's got time and motion study charts showing that if you hold your glass in your right hand and the bottle in your left you'll have time for twenty per cent more drinks before the bar closes. Or something. Anyway, Captain S/M has told us all to get our Maintenance Weeks organised instead of having the usual shambles.'

The rest of the wardroom looked sceptical. The Submarine Service had been trying to organise its Maintenance Weeks since the first of the Holland boats went to sea at the turn of the century.

'*So*,' The Bodger went on, 'seeing as how it's Monday morning, I thought we might have a conference and see if we can fix everything to happen at different times instead of in one Godalmighty chaos. It shouldn't be too difficult. Now . . . What have we got on this week? Number One?'

Looking like a man upon whom great issues hung, Wilfred took out the desk diary which he kept hidden in his drawer. He began to read from it in a hollow voice, as though chanting a rubric for lost souls.

'Paint ship, sir. Twelve bodies overdue for the escape tank. They've got to requalify this week. Five blokes for X-rays. Another six to have a first-aid course. Store ship for six weeks at sea. Survey all emergency stores. Send all the bunk covers and curtains to the cleaners. Get Chippy to mend the cupboards in the Petty Officers' mess. Muster all the attractive items in the permanent loan list. Fix up the ship's company run ashore to Brighton. Captain S/M's rounds of the messdeck inboard.'

'Fine, *fine*,' said The Bodger. 'I can see you've got a pretty busy week.' It was a long time since The Bodger had been First Lieutenant of a running submarine and he had forgotten how many details had to be arranged.

'How about you, Chief?'

Derek opened a huge blue file marked 'Engineer Officer—Very Urgent' and found among the papers, drawings and stores notes which overflowed from it a piece of paper covered in figures and squiggly drawings.

'The starboard supercharger was rumbling on the way in, sir. We'll have to strip that down and have a look at it. The main engine lub-oil's due for a change. We'll have to fuel and take on fresh water some time this week. We're docking on Thursday to fit that new echo-sounder for the boffins. And we've got to change the after periscope . . .'

'Fine, fine, fine,' The Bodger said hurriedly. Talking to technical officers on technical subjects always gave The Bodger a feeling closely resembling vertigo. He nerved himself again.

'How about you, Dagwood?'

'The radar bioscope was on the blink on the way back, sir. And we've got to charge sometime this week. We're fitting a new whip aerial and there's our side of the echo-sounder to fit and test. . . .'

'Rusty?'

'Load three fish on Wednesday, sir. All the sonar ratings are due for another ear test. We need some more smoke candles. *Terrapin* have challenged us at cricket, sir. . . .'

'Pilot?'

'New chart folios, sir, and a new ensign if we can get it. That one's getting a bit crabby. Change binoculars. They're all flooded. We've got to swing compasses again some time before we leave, sir. . . .'

'Have *you* got anything on, Mid?'

'I must get some more films, sir. Everybody's seen the ones we've got. And we need some more squash and lime juice. . . .'

'*Well.*' The Bodger was slightly taken aback by the multitude of requirements *Seahorse* must fulfil before she was ready for sea again.

'Let's not get down-hearted, men. Let's say we do the charge tomorrow, load fish on Wednesday, swing compasses on Thursday . . .'

'But we're going into dock on Thursday, sir.'

'So we are. All right, let's do the charge *today* . . . God.' The Bodger stopped, aghast. 'I've just remembered. This morning is the only time we can have the Attack Teacher.' The Bodger looked at his watch. 'And we should have been up there five minutes ago! I'll go and tell them we're still coming. . . .'

The Bodger sprang from his chair.

'Get the Attack Team together as soon as you can,' he said to Wilfred over his shoulder as he went.

There was a short silence in the wardroom after the Bodger's passing.

117

'So much for work-studying our Maintenance Week,' said Dagwood, at last.

The wardroom had no more time to ponder upon work study. Messengers from all over the establishment were already queueing up outside. The telephone rang continually.

'First Lieutenant, sir? The Sick Bay say can they have the ratings for X-rays now, sir? It's the only time the Barracks can take them.'

'Engineer Officer, sir? The Spare Gear Officer inboard says would you send up two hands to collect some gear, sir. . . .'

Each message drained away a little of *Seahorse's* effective force. By ten o'clock, Derek found himself quite alone. The other officers were in the attack team and the ship's company had scattered like autumn leaves. When Derek poked his head out of the wardroom, the control room was empty. The whole submarine, in either direction, was empty.

'Anybody there?'

Derek's voice echoed along the deserted passageway.

'Hello? Anybody there?'

'Sorr?'

A head projected from the door of the stokers' mess.

'Gotobed, it's nice to see you!'

'Want somethin', sorr?'

'No no, Gotobed, it's just nice to hear another human voice, that's all.'

Derek sat down again in the wardroom, full of warm thoughts towards Stoker Gotobed. He was enormously cheered to know that there was somebody else there.

Derek's feelings towards Gotobed would have surprised a stranger to *Seahorse*, because Gotobed was not a man of prepossessing appearance. His face, chest and most of his body were covered in a tangle of thick black hair. His arms hung down to his knees. In repose—his favourite position—he looked like a successful mutation of man and ape.

Gotobed was long overdue for a move to another submarine, but Derek had fought off all attempts to have him drafted because Gotobed was the one man in *Seahorse* who was irreplaceable. Other stokers could be relieved. Derek could be relieved. The Captain himself could be relieved. Gotobed could not. Gotobed was the only man living who could work the Oily Bilge Pump.

Seahorse's Oily Bilge Pump was a piece of machinery which defied the normal principles of mechanical science. On the shop floor it passed all tests imposed upon it, but as soon as it was fitted into the submarine, it became possessed by devils. Dockyard workmen had wept salt tears over it. The makers' representatives had spent sleepless nights by its side. A succession of engineer officers from various submarines and surface ships had tried out every combination of its valves. But the Oily Bilge Pump refused to take a suction for anyone but Gotobed. When anyone else but Gotobed tried to use the pump it not only refused to take a suction but sprayed its compartment with bilge water. Gotobed was therefore as vital to *Seahorse* as her pressure hull.

Derek's pleasant meditations upon Gotobed and his indispensability were suddenly interrupted.

'Excuse me . . .'

Derek looked up. A young man in clean white overalls, carrying a brief-case, stood in the doorway. He wore two stop-watches slung on lanyards round his neck. In one top pocket he carried a row of pencils and in the other a small slide rule. His eyes burned meanwhile with the fierce fanatic glare of a reformer.

Derek recognised the face at once. This was the keen young scientist in the advertisements for chemical products, the successful business executive advising his less successful colleague to change his brand of tobacco, the wholesome salesman soothing the nervous housewife's fears.

'I'm from the Work Study Team.'

'Oh. Well, come in. What can we do for you?'

'We've been asked to do a survey on the way submarines plan their maintenance periods.'

'Really? Well, when you find out, let me know, will you? I've been in submarines nine years and I've never managed to plan a maintenance period yet.'

The Work Study Man smiled. 'That's exactly why we have work study. Frankly, you know, you need it . . .'

'Do we?'

'Yes. Do you know, we did a short survey on *Terrapin* last month and we found that the average time worked by each man per day was *two hours*!'

'Blimey,' said Derek. 'The Lamm of God must have been cracking the whip! Did she go to sea all right?'

'Yes.'

'Did she come back again?'

'Yes, but . . .'

'Obviously two hours a day was enough then.'

The Work Study Man smiled again. Overcoming the subject's prejudices was Lesson One, Line One in the Work Study syllabus.

'Let me show you some of the results we've achieved . . .'

'Oh no, please don't bother,' Derek protested. 'You just crack on and do whatever you have to do. Don't mind me. . . .'

But the Work Study Man had already, in two economical movements, unzipped his brief-case and whipped out a large drawing.

'Here are some of the surveys we've done. You can see that in the case of a large shore establishment we cut the pay office staff by fourteen officers and thirty-seven ratings, merely by replanning their office layout. We cut the maintenance time on the potato-peeler in a cruiser by nearly seventy-five per cent! On one air station we cut the rum issue time by a half . . .'

'Just a minute,' said Derek, his argumentative instincts rising, 'that may be all right in industry but not in the Navy. What exactly have you achieved?'

'What have we achieved? An enormous saving in . . .'

'Let's just take the examples you've given me. You've cut the staff in some wretched pay office by umpteen blokes. But what's happened to those blokes? They haven't gone outside. They're not civilians. The Navy's still paying them. They're probably settled in some *other* pay office right now and when you come to work study *that* pay office you're going to find some familiar faces. And they're going to hate you. And the chaps who save all that time on the spud-peeler. What do you think they're going to do with that extra time? Maintain more spud-peelers? Not likely! I'll tell you what they're going to do. They're going to have time for two cigarettes instead of one. And as for *cutting the time of the rum issue by half*. . . Do you think the Navy's going to thank you for that? Why, it doesn't bear thinking about! It would be like missing out every other bar of the National Anthem!'

As Derek finished his rhetoric he realised that it had all been wasted. The Work Study Man was still talking.

'. . . And so the best thing would be for me to take one of your ratings and plot his daily work.'

'You want one of our blokes to work-study?' The idea struck Derek with such force that he blinked.

'*Gotobed!*'

'Sorr?'

Gotobed's massive face appeared at the wardroom door.

'Gotobed, this gentleman would like to work study you.'

'Sorr,' said Gotobed blankly.

The Work Study Man was already writing in his notebook.

'Gotobed,' he said briskly. 'Right. What's your job, Gotobed?'

'Ah gits a soction on the bliddy bilges with the bliddy pomp, sorr.'

The Work Study Man paused. 'I *beg* your pardon?'

'He pumps out the engine room and motor room bilges,' said Derek.

'I see. Is that all?'

'It's quite enough.'

'I see. Well, this should make a very good subject. A fairly simple operation with clearly defined movements.'

Derek kept his face expressionless. 'Off you go, Gotobed. Pump out the engine room and motor room bilges. This gentleman will go with you.'

Gotobed led the way aft to the small pump space which contained the Oily Bilge Pump. It was Gotobed's own compartment; he was responsible for its cleanliness. It was his shrine. Gotobed climbed down while the Work Study Man started a stop-watch and made symbols in his notebook.

Gotobed's performance was well worth a few symbols. He primed the air pump with water from a small can, blew some drops of water from the filling hole, replaced the cap and sealed it with two mighty strokes of a hammer.

A faint frown appeared on the Work Study Man's brow.

Humming tonelessly between his teeth, Gotobed climbed out of the pump space and shambled along the engine room to the first bilge suction valve which he opened one turn. Returning to the pump, he placed his shoulder against the motor casing and shoved, at the same time turning the starting rheostat one notch.

The Oily Bilge Pump started with an eerie whistling noise which made the hair on the back of the Work Study Man's neck rise involuntarily. The whistling note deepened to a whirring and then to a steady roar. The pump began to give spasmodic shudders which Gotobed met with timed shoulder heaves, crouching by the pump as though assisting a cow in labour.

'Bliddy pomp's got a bliddy wackum!'

'What's that?'

'Bliddy wackum!'

'*Eh?*'

'Wackum wackum wackum!' roared Gotobed over the booming pump. The vacuum gauge quivered wildly, whereupon Gotobed released the pump, hoisted himself out of the compartment, ran to the bilge suction, opened it fully, and dropped down again into the pump space. Once there, he raised a foot, placed it firmly against the pump casing and thrust. The pump gave several more shudders and settled down to a steady contented hum. The Oily Bilge Pump was taking a suction from the bilges.

Derek had strolled aft to watch the show.

'How's it going?' he asked the Work Study Man.

The Work Study Man's face was transfigured with holy rapture.

'It's a classic! This is a natural for the Society! It'll

make my reputation! I don't know if you realise it but people will talk about this in years to come!'

'Glad to hear it,' said Derek politely.

'I've counted sixty-two separate wasted motions! The whole thing has taken thirteen minutes twenty seconds. I can see at a glance we can get down to five movements and anything over three minutes would be a criminal waste of time!'

'I'd like to see you do it quicker. In fact I'd like to see you get a suction at all.'

'You can't be serious!'

'I most certainly *am*!'

'I don't believe it.'

'You just have a try. I'll tell you this much. I can't do it.'

'But I don't know where the . . . where anything is. . . .'

'You tell us when to do it, and we'll do everything for you.'

The Work Study Man climbed down and gingerly started the pump. It started immediately with an ugly howling noise as though the pump casing contained a man-eating animal.

'Open the suction!'

The pump gave a series of seismic palpitations and then exploded. Derek leaned over and looked through the hatch. He could see nothing in the fine oily mist which was rising from the compartment.

'I should stop the pump now,' he said. 'I've got a towel in the wardroom.'

Gotobed stopped the pump. 'Too much bliddy wackum,' he said disgustedly.

*   *   *

When the Bodger and the others returned just before lunch The Bodger said: 'Before I forget, Chief, we've got a work study man coming down to see us some time today. You'd better look after him.'

'He's been, sir. And gone.'

'Already? Did he enjoy himself?'

'I think so, sir.'

'So much for work study then.'

10

The Submarine Staff Office was, architecturally, an undistinguished room. Only two chairs were provided, one for Commander S/M and the other for Lieutenant-Commander Barney Lightfoot, resident staff officer; submarine captains, visitors and onlookers all stood. On one wall were bunches of signals and a map of the English Channel; on another, a large board on which were chalked the dates individual submarines were due for various commitments. Above Commander S/M's desk were the two mandatory staff notices 'Next Week, We Must Get Organised' and 'Haven't You Heard? It's All Been Changed.' Above the desk of Barney Lightfoot, an erudite man, was a typewritten notice: 'If you can keep your head when all about you are losing theirs, it means you haven't the vaguest idea what's happening.'

Nevertheless, the Staff Office was, if the term could be used in its loosest sense, the nerve centre of the squadron. It was simultaneously an operations room, a club-house, and a coffee-bar. There Captain S/M kept his finger on the squadron pulse. There Commander S/M grappled with insoluble logistical problems, and there the squadron technical officers explained to sceptical audiences that their men were only possessed of two arms each and each day contained a maximum of twenty-four hours. There also, the submarine captains attempted to keep up with the latest changes in events.

'Have you met your Boffin yet?' Commander S/M asked The Bodger as he arrived one morning.

'What Boffin?'

'The one you're taking with you. The one you docked *specially* to fit an echo-sounder for.'

'He's not coming until tomorrow.'

'It's all been changed. He's joining you this morning and he's going to stay with you for about two months, while you amble down to the Equator and take a few readings for him. Don't ask me what sort of readings. I was on the blower to Barwick & Todhunters last night and they say they're sending someone who's been in submarines before. So he should be fairly well house-trained.'

Barwick & Todhunter's representative could fairly be described as house-trained. He was at that moment standing at the end of *Seahorse's* gangway, waiting for the stream of sailors carrying bags of potatoes to die down so that he could cross himself. He himself carried a small hold-all bag and a slightly larger black box. He was dressed in a black jacket, striped trousers, an Old Harrovian tie, a white carnation in his button-hole and a black homburg hat. On raising his hat as he stepped on to *Seahorse's* casing he revealed smoothly brushed blond hair, a pink complexion and an air of politely-concealed dismay. He gave Wilfred, who met him on the casing, the impression that he had come expecting to stay for the week-end but had, by some monstrous social mischance, mistaken the time, the date, and the place. He shook hands with Wilfred warmly and produced a card.

'Mr Lancelot Sudbury-Dunne.'

'How do you do' said Wilfred. 'I'm the First Lieutenant.'

Wilfred eyed the small hold-all bag and the black box. 'Is this all you've got?'

'Yes,' said Mr Sudbury-Dunne. 'And it's quite enough, I think, to take in a submarine, don't you?'

'Why yes,' said Wilfred. 'I'm sorry I sounded surprised. It's just that the last, um . . .'

'Boffin?' enquired Mr Sudbury-Dunne.

'. . . bloke we took to sea arrived twenty minutes before we sailed with seventeen packing cases of stuff. And when we got to sea he announced that he wanted three holes drilled in the pressure hull.'

'How trying for you.'

'If you'll just leave your stuff there I'll get a sailor to take it down to the wardroom for you.'

'Oh, don't bother,' said Mr Sudbury-Dunne and collecting his bag and his box he slid through the fore hatch like an eel. It struck Wilfred that they had been given something extraordinary in the way of boffins.

'I'm afraid the Captain's not here yet,' Wilfred said, after he had introduced Mr Sudbury-Dunne to the rest of the officers. 'He should be down very shortly.'

'Good. I'm anxious to meet him.' Mr Sudbury-Dunne was well aware that the Captain's personality was of considerable importance to his experiments. He knew that his own presence had been imposed upon the ship and he would be a guest of the wardroom for two months. A hostile or even an uninterested captain could seriously hamper his work.

The Bodger was just as anxious to meet The Boffin. 'I hope to God he's not one of these pale-faced state-scholarship trogs who puke all over the wardroom table and tell me I'm running my ship all wrong.' The Bodger knew that he was stuck with this boffin for two months. 'If you get up one morning and don't like an officer's face you can tell him to go away and put a turk's head on it and paint it yellow. But with a boffin you've got to be polite, if only for the sake of the Navy Estimates.'

In the event, neither need have worried.

'Bodger!'

'Dan!'

Mr Lancelot Sudbury-Dunne was no ordinary boffin. He was an old friend and drinking partner of The Bodger's. They had once suffered together under Black Sebastian. In spite of his faultless social appearance, Mr Lancelot Sudbury-Dunne was a man after The Bodger's own heart, so much so that he had earned the nickname of Dangerous Dan. The wardroom were greatly relieved to hear it. Plainly Dangerous Dan could be told to take his face away and put a turk's head on it and paint it yellow, just like anyone else.

The Bodger was delighted to see his friend again and a little remorseful over his remarks about boffins.

'I take back all I said about boffins, Dan,' he said.

'That's all right, Bodger. We're a pretty thick-skinned lot.' Dangerous Dan, on his part, was just as pleased to see The Bodger, although he was secretly overawed by The Bodger's present status as the commanding officer of a modern submarine.

'If it wasn't for that dirty laugh, Bodger, I would hardly recognise you,' he said. 'You're looking so prosperous! Shades of Black Sebastian. He didn't hold out much prospect for the future for either of us, did he?'

'As a submariner,' The Bodger quoted, from memory, 'this officer is earnestly recommended for duties with the Fleet Air Arm. That's what he wrote about me! But to get back to the main thing Dan, what exactly do you want us to do on this trip?'

'Well, it's like this.' Dangerous Dan's manner became precise and business-like. 'As you probably know, everybody is looking for the big technical break-through in submarine detection, though nobody knows what form it will take yet. But first of all, we've got to know a lot more about the sea itself. After all, if you were hunting leopard or something you would be a bloody fool if you didn't take the trouble to find out about the sort of country where it lived. And so with submarines. Do you know, most of the earth's surface is covered in water and we know almost damn all about it! Just take the average chart. Have you got a chart handy, Pilot?'

'Any particular chart, sir?' said Gavin.

'Any one will do and I'm Dangerous Dan to you.'

'O.K., Dan.' Gavin went to his locker and pulled out the first chart which came to his hand. It was a small-scale chart of the Western Approaches.

'Just the job,' Dangerous Dan said briskly. 'Now, just look at all these soundings here. They look impressive enough and obviously someone in the past has been to a lot of trouble getting them. But as you go more than a hundred miles or so from land the soundings are spread out in lines, each sounding miles from the next one and each line miles from the next line. Anything might be happening between those soundings. It's like trying to find your way through a dark wood using every other eye once every quarter of an hour. Then there's tides. You all know that the tidal streams the average Joe uses on the surface bear no relation at all to the tides at five hundred feet or even at a hundred feet. In the Straits of Gibraltar for example, there are two or three different streams all on top of each other.'

'I know just what you mean,' said the Bodger. 'Do you remember that time with Black Sebastian when we'd been dived for hours and hours and I was trying to make a landfall on the Needles? I can still hear his voice when he looked through the periscope. "Pass the message to the Navigating Officer, Portland Bill loud and clear dead ahead!" '

Dangerous Dan chuckled. 'I believe Black Sebastian was a little shaken himself. It's to try and avoid that sort of thing that we're making this trip. What we're trying to get is a three-D, wide screen, stereophonic picture of the sea. It'll take years to do, of course, and I have a nasty feeling we haven't got years to do it in, but anyway Bodger, *I'll* be doing all the work. Even I haven't got anything to do until we get down to the Equator. It should be a bit of a jolly for you lot.'

Seahorse sailed on a calm summer evening, with St Catherin's light winking in the dusk and the lights of passing ships glowing like jewels. The engines threw out two long trails of vapour which lay on the water without dispersing. Overhead, the stars lit the sky down to the horizon where the red glow of the sun still lingered. It was the weather the sailor knows as 'Signing-On Weather.'

Gavin read the weather reports and prophesied a falling barometer, high seas and head winds but day after day the miraculous weather persisted. As the reports deteriorated, the weather improved. Each morning the sun rose behind a shining veil of low cloud, shone all day in a cloudless sky, and set in a spectacular display of colour.

'If you saw that on a postcard,' Dagwood said of one sunset, 'you'd call the artist a liar.'

The Bay of Biscay was like a plain of mobile glass, with a long swell running from the Atlantic. *Seahorse* rose and dipped steadily, the water foaming and tumbling off her bows and washing along the ballast tanks. The sea seemed to have a hypnotic effect upon Dangerous Dan. He spent hours at a time studying the water welling up and pouring away again, his eyes fixed on the changing surface of the sea as though he were already trying to penetrate its depths.

The Bodger made his landfall on the Canaries at dawn. The islands appeared magically through the morning mist, their heads wreathed in thin layers of cloud and their bases jutting suddenly from the sea, like the bastions and turrets of a sorcerer's castle. It did not seem possible that such islands could be inhabited by humans; they were more like the homes of fairies who played in the gardens which had once tempted Hercules.

Seahorse fuelled and collected mail at Las Palmas and then set out for the tropical Atlantic. There, it was as though the sea claimed the ship for its own. Dolphins shot up and over in beautiful curves through the wake. The startling water spouts of whales appeared on the beam. Flying fish hopped and scattered at the bows and sea-birds swooped, wailing and watchful, around the bridge. At night *Seahorse* swam through a milky sea of phosphorescence. Fire streamed along the hull leaving sparks which still shone after the wave had receded. The bow wave was an ever-renewing ridge of silver light which flashed and sparkled as it broke and opened out from the ship.

Down below, the ship's company passed the time between watches sleeping, arguing and playing crib, draughts or uckers. The morning rum issue, the afternoon sleep and the evening film-show were the main events of the day. The Petty Officer Telegraphist produced a daily news sheet from the B.B.C. but the items seemed to the men in *Seahorse* to come from another world; it was difficult to relate the events described in them to *Seahorse*, a solitary ship upon a wide sea.

The wardroom grew tired of uckers and tried Monopoly but after the Midshipman had won the first three games The Bodger banned it as bad for discipline.

'I'm not going to have my wardroom's morale undermined by a bloody stupid parlour game,' he said. 'Besides, Mid, it brings out all your worst instincts.'

The wardroom returned to uckers, where The Bodger was on more familiar ground. Uckers bore a family resemblance to ludo but Submarine Uckers, and particularly The Bodger's Uckers, was to ludo as National League baseball is to girls' school rounders. It was a merciless game. It was mandatory to sneer at a losing opponent and to accuse a winner of cheating. The game lent itself to psychological warfare. Innuendo and insult could reduce an opponent to a state where he could barely bring himself to pick up the dice. The Bodger and Dangerous Dan were experts.

Dangerous Dan introduced the wardroom to Chinese Chess. The winner was he who manœuvred his opponent into taking the last match from three piles of varying size. Dangerous Dan won so consistently that The Bodger insisted on an explanation. The solution, expressed in binary notation, left the Bodger as baffled as before. Dangerous Dan took on the whole wardroom at Fan Tan, selling them the pack for a penny a card and paying tenpence for every card they succeeded in laying out. The wardroom only desisted when they had lost most of the remainder of their month's pay and the ship's welfare fund was beginning to be in jeopardy.

Dangerous Dan was the complete gamesman. Even Dagwood, the wardroom's acknowledged conversationalist, could not outploy him.

'You may be right,' said Dangerous Dan, while they were discussing road traffic. 'I can only repeat what the Minister of Transport said to me. . . .'

'I've always regretted,' he said, when they were discussing Lawrence, 'that he didn't sign my copy of *Lady Chatterley* for me. . . .'

When the conversation ranged as far as Freud and Jung, Dangerous Dan clinched the social aspects of psychology with: 'I've always been told that an *introvert* marries the first girl who'll sleep with him and an *extrovert* marries the first girl who won't.'

Though over-shadowed by Dangerous Dan in the broader issues, Dagwood had one particular game which he had perfected himself. It was called the Needle Game and was played between two players, Dagwood and his victim. The rules were simple. Dagwood won if he succeeded in provoking his opponent into a display of bad-temper or, better still, rage. His opponent won if he kept his temper.

Dagwood often tried Derek, though he was too amiable to make a good opponent. But Derek did have two *bêtes noire* on which he could be relied upon to comment strongly. One was Planned Maintenance, and the other Work Study.

'We don't seem to get much time for maintenance these days, do we, Derek?' Dagwood remarked casually after lunch one day.

Derek raised his head warily from his pillow, like a bull catching the first sight of an intruder far away on the other side of the meadow.

'What do you mean?'

'Well, I mean they never seem to give us any time to. . .'

Derek rose like a game-fish. 'We'll never get submarine maintenance periods on a basis until they become a submarine commitment, like an exercise. The date of something like 'Lucky Alphonse' is sacred. Why shouldn't a maintenance period be sacred as well? We should be like the air boys. If an aircraft's routines are not up to date, it just doesn't fly. If the day ever comes when a submarine is not allowed to *dive* because it's routines are not up to date, *then* we'd see a difference! But it won't happen. They arrange the programme first and any gaps they find they give to maintenance. Now shut up Dagwood and let me get some sleep for God's sake. . . .'

Dagwood chalked up the exchange as a draw and lay in wait for his favourite opponent—Wilfred.

Wilfred was almost impregnable as far as the Needle Game was concerned but he had one vulnerable spot. As First Lieutenant, Wilfred was responsible for the sailors' food. In practice the Coxswain ordered, administered and mustered the food but in theory Wilfred was the ship's catering officer and responsible to the Captain. Wilfred took his supervisory duties very seriously.

On the day *Seahorse* crossed the Tropic of Cancer it was unfortunate that the Coxswain provided Olde Englishe pudding for lunch. When Dagwood was given his portion, he held up his hand.

'Anything the matter, sir?' said the Steward.

'Hark,' said Dagwood.

Wilfred was still smarting from the previous tea-time when Dagwood had looked at the butter and said 'C'est magnifique, mais ce n'est pas le beurre!'

'*Now* what's the matter?' he said sourly.

'What's the matter, Dagwood?' The Bodger asked. The exchanges between Dagwood and Wilfred had often lightened his day.

'I hear the Muse, sir. She's calling to me, in accents soft and low.'

'What's she saying?'

'The usual drivel, I expect,' said Wilfred.

'She's saying . . . One moment . . . Yes, here it is . . . It's a poem, sir. She's saying,

> Despite the many moans you hear:
> There's one you all forget.
> Though Christmas came but once *last* year,
> The pudding's with us yet!'

It was a bull's-eye in one shot. Wilfred glowered, while the rest of the wardroom hooted. Nevertheless The Bodger thought it a little unfair. In spite of their difficulties in storing and cooking a variety of food in a confined space and in a hot climate, The Bodger thought that Wilfred, the Coxswain and the Chef were doing very well. In the circumstances, The Bodger was quite satisfied. The Bodger's main concern was not what the ship's company should eat, but what they should drink. There would soon be a shortage of fresh water on board. *Seahorse's* tanks did not contain enough water for a prolonged passage in the tropics. There was a distiller but it was fitted in the main passageway and the noise and heat it generated made the messes adjacent to it uninhabitable. The only solution was a compromise, to run the

136

distiller for limited periods and to ration fresh water. Otherwise, the problem seemed insoluble without divine intervention.

Unknown to The Bodger, divine intervention was almost at hand. That evening, soon after tea, *Seahorse* ran into a tropical rainstorm. The Midshipman was on watch and knew exactly what to do.

'Close up radar. Tell the Captain.'

The messenger found The Bodger with Dangerous Dan in the petty officers' mess, playing the final of the ship's uckers tournament against the Chief Stoker and the Second Coxswain.

'From the bridge sir, he's closing up radar, sir.'

'What for?'

'I think it's a rain cloud, sir. . . .'

'*Rain!*'

The Midshipman pointed out the cloud to The Bodger.

'I'm closing up radar, sir, because of the likelihood of reduced visibility forrard sir. . . .'

'To hell with radar and to hell with the reduced vis! It's the rain I'm after!'

The cloud was only four or five miles ahead of the ship. A curtain of rain was lashing the sea over a front of several miles. *Seahorse* was heading directly for the centre of the storm. The Bodger moistened parched lips and rubbed the stubble on his chin.

'It's like an answer to prayer,' he whispered. He bent to the voice-pipe. 'Pass the message to all compartments, all ratings not on watch muster on the casing with soap for showers.'

'Say again, sir!' yelled Ripper, who was on the wheel.

'*Clear lower deck! Muster on the casing! Provide Soap!*'

'Clear lower deck, muster on the casing, provide soap, aye aye, sir!' shouted Ripper. 'The Captain's gone off his rocker,' he added to the Radio Electrician, who was petty officer of the watch. The Radio Electrician nodded sombrely.

In a short time over sixty naked men, clutching soap and sponges expectantly, mustered on the casing and gazed at the approaching storm.

Wearing only his soap-bag in one hand, The Bodger conned the ship towards the centre of the storm.

'Starboard five . . . Steady . . . Steer that . . . That should do it. . . .'

With a booming roar of wind the storm was upon them. The rain drummed on the casing and bounced off the sailors' naked bodies. *Seahorse* was enveloped in a grey wall of water. The sailors pounded their chests and shouted songs as they leisurely soaped themselves for their first real wash since the ship left England.

Dangerous Dan joined the crowd on the casing and began to wash himself like a man demented. He scrubbed and rubbed himself as though every second were priceless. His energy amused the sailors who were covering themselves in lather and allowing the blessed rain to wash it off.

But there was method in Dangerous Dan's frenzied washing. The rain storm passed away as quickly as it had come. The rain stopped abruptly. The uncovered sun began to harden the outer layers of lather. The Bodger seized the voice-pipe in a desperate, slippery hand.

'After that cloud! Hard a starboard! Full ahead together!'

Seahorse heeled in a tight turn towards the retreating storm. Her half-lathered officers and ship's company watched her progress anxiously. The artificer on watch in the engine room was advised of the emergency. The engines thundered as they had never thundered before.

Directed by a wild-eyed Bodger, *Seahorse* dodged all over the ocean but the storm eddied this way and that, steadily gaining distance from the pursuing submarine. At last The Bodger was forced to abandon the chase.

Dangerous Dan was conspicuous amongst the throng on the casing. He was as sleek and shining as a seal.

'I must say I admire your soap,' he said to Dagwood, whose body and hair were still partly covered in encrusted lather. 'What sort is it?'

Dangerous Dan had his own version of the Needle Game.

Dangerous Dan began his survey when *Seahorse* was sixty miles from the Equator. Dangerous Dan working was quite a different man from Dangerous Dan amusing himself with party games on passage. He was up every morning at five o'clock to calibrate his instruments and he did not finish his last calculations on the day's data until after midnight. He had placed the black box on the chart-table but the main part of his equipment including the echo-sounder had been installed in a space between the Coxswain's store and the oilskin locker. Dangerous Dan's working day was spent bobbing and ducking between the control room and the store.

Seahorse dived twice a day for Dangerous Dan's readings, while the Black Box in the control room gave an instantaneous three-dimensional picture of the sea bottom, computed from the echo-sounder transmissions.

The Black Box was the most fascinating side-show

anyone in *Seahorse* had ever seen. The ship's company queued up to look at it.

'Roll up, roll up. What The Butler Saw Twenty Thousand Leagues Under The Sea,' Leading Seaman Gorbles said.

'Is *that* the bottom of the sea?' exclaimed the Chef. 'Blimey, I thought it was flat!'

The Chef spoke for most of the ship's company. If anyone in *Seahorse* had ever thought about the sea bottom at all, they had imagined it sloping downwards from the continents to a flat plain until it sloped upwards again for the next continent—with the odd uncharted pinnacle regularly rammed by submarines off Londonderry. Dangerous Dan's Black Box showed that the sea had a geography of its own. *Seahorse* swam suspended over submarine mountain ranges which would have dwarfed the Alps and over deeps which could easily have contained the Grand Canyon. The Black Box showed a panorama of drowned rivers winding through ancient courses on the sea floor, islands which had been cut off in their growth towards the light, plains as wide as the steppes and foothills which stretched like the folds of a giant's blanket for hundreds of miles. The instrument was also sensitive enough to record objects between *Seahorse* and the sea floor. Strange vast shadows like clouds moved over the screen, marking the passage of a shoal of an unimaginable number of fish. Sometimes the screen picked up speeding images with spiked tails which looked as though sea-dragons on a titanic scale were flying over the landscape below them.

As Dangerous Dan's experiments progressed, every man in *Seahorse* began to have an inkling of the immensity of the ocean. The sea was not a homogeneous mass of water but had currents, like veins, and layers, like muscles.

It was always in a state of stress, a shifting, restless, hostile entity. *Seahorse* was an intruder, creeping about on the fringe of a colossal mystery and peering, from an impertinent distance, at the supreme wonder of the earth.

The Bodger maintained the normal sonar listening watch while *Seahorse* was dived for the experimental runs. Although *Seahorse* was so far off the main shipping routes that there was never any ships' hydrophone effect, the sea itself provided a miscellany of sounds which descended through the whole range of human hearing. There was often a hollow resonant booming, like the pounding of mammoth breakers a thousand miles away, coupled with clicks, thumps, metallic knocking and shrill cat calls. Porpoise wailed near the surface and at every depth there came suddenly a deafening staccato chatter, like the applause of a myriad scaly claws.

'Whoever said this was the silent world needs his head examined,' said Leading Seaman Gorbles. 'More like Marble Arch on a Sunday.'

One morning Leading Seaman Gorbles picked up a new sound. It was a slow eerie beat, accompanied by regular high-pitched squeals. He pointed it out to Rusty, who was officer of the watch. Rusty called The Bodger, who listened himself.

'What do you make of it, Gorbles?'

'Couldn't say, sir. Could be transmissions, though they're nothing like anything I've ever heard before. Sounds like someone having a cheap thrill, sir.'

'Put it over the control room broadcast. And don't be facetious.'

The control room was filled with the treble squeaks, underlined by the same slow steady beat. The sound had an artificial regularity, without the haphazardness of a sound emitted by a living organism.

Dangerous Dan paused on his way down to the store to listen. Wilfred and Dagwood came out of the wardroom.

'Very slow revs, sir. Not more than twenty a minute. Sometimes not even that, sir.'

The Bodger made up his mind.

'Action Stations! Attack team close up!'

11

The Admiralty's orders on the action to be taken by a captain on gaining an unidentified and possibly hostile submarine contact were contained in a Top Secret file in the Captain's safe. But The Bodger did not need to consult them. He already knew their general gist almost by heart. Behind the veiled diplomatic language and the ambiguous official wording, they were quite explicit; they could be summed up in the traditional phrase 'Engage the enemy more closely'.

Although the ship's company had been told nothing of the position, the attack team closed up as quickly as though the Admiral himself were watching them. In *Seahorse*, as in all operational submarines, the step from peace to war was a short one. Leading Seaman Gorbles' reports began to come over the action broadcast with a decisive snap which he had never achieved in fleet exercises.

'Target three two three . . . Moving left. . . .'

The Chef stuck his head out of the galley as the rest of the attack team tumbled by to their action stations.

'Where's the fire?'

'Haven't you heard, Whacker,' said the Steward. 'We're at war with the whales.'

'Less noise,' said the Bodger. 'Assume quiet state.'

It was as though The Bodger had given *Seahorse* the order to die. In a few minutes all inessential fans and motors had been stopped, the telegraph order bells had been muffled, Derek stopped one shaft and the submarine glided on at slow speed. *Seahorse* became as quiet as a hunting cat, ears cocked for the least sound.

Suddenly, with the violence of a thunder-clap, there was a loud clang and an oath from the direction of the engine room. The Bodger jumped in spite of himself.

'Tell that rating to come here!'

A shame-faced stoker appeared in the control room.

'What was that noise?'

'I dropped a spanner, sir.'

'You and your chums back in your ivory tower don't seem to realise that there is someone *out there*,' The Bodger pointed dramatically at the bulkhead, 'just listening for crumbs like you. Now get out! And take your shoes off!'

'. . . Target faded, sir.'

'Hah, he's heard us. I'm not surprised. I expect they can hear us back in Pompey with all the noise we're making. Bring all after tubes to the action state.'

The Bodger regretted his outburst almost as soon as he had finished it. He remembered that the ship's company had not been told anything yet. He picked up the broadcast microphone and pressed the button. There was no hum from the system. Just as The Bodger was gathering breath to vent his irritation, Dagwood said: 'The broadcast system is switched off for quiet state, sir.'

The Bodger let out his breath again in a long sigh. 'Switch it on again while I talk to the ship's company.'

'Aye aye, sir.'

'Main broadcast switched on, sir.'

'D'you hear there. This is the Captain speaking. We

144

have a Visitor. About ten minutes ago we got an un-identified contact on sonar. I don't know what it is yet but I will let you know as soon as I do. The attack team will remain closed up in the meantime. That's all.'

'All after tubes in the action state, sir.'

'Very good.'

'Visitor regained, sir, one five seven. . . .'

'One five seven!' The target had gone round nearly a hundred and eighty degrees, unheard by sonar. The Bodger gritted his teeth, feeling the temper rising in him.

'One five eight, moving right, faint *ecstatic* trans-missions. . . .'

'What do you mean "*ecstatic*"?'

'Can't describe it any other way, sir,' replied Leading Seaman Gorbles apologetically. 'Sounds like someone enjoying himself, sir. Can't get a transmission interval or nothing on him, sir.'

It was the strangest attack The Bodger had ever carried out. The Visitor appeared to track steadily right, then stop, track back, and shoot suddenly forward again.

'What speed does the plot give?'

'Last speed five knots, sir, mean speed *forty* knots, sir!'

'*Impossible!*'

'That's what the plot says, sir,' said the Signalman, aggrievedly.

'Check that, Number One.'

Wilfred measured the Signalman's angles and made a rough calculation.

'It certainly seems like that, sir.'

'It *can't* be!'

'. . . Visitor faded, last bearing two one one. . . .'

'Now we'll have to wait, I suppose,' The Bodger said. 'And see where he pops up again next time.'

Dangerous Dan was watching the attack from the

tactful safety of the wardroom door. The science of submarine versus submarine attacking had been in its infancy when he left submarines just after the war and he was enthralled by his first privileged view of it. Dangerous Dan knew enough of submarine tactics to appreciate that the procedure he was now watching was as far removed from the normal submarine attack on a surface vessel as higher mathematics was from mental arithmetic. As a submariner himself, Dangerous Dan could guess at the ordeal The Bodger was undergoing. Engaging an unknown submarine was difficult enough; engaging one which behaved so unpredictably was like going out to catch a criminal who was not only waving a meat-axe but fighting drunk.

'. . . Visitor regained. Zero zero eight. . . .'

'Gone through a hundred and eighty degrees again,' said The Bodger.

'. . . Visitor bearing steady. . . .'

'Plot suggests target turned towards, sir!' cried Wilfred.

'Full ahead together! *Hard* a port!'

'All round H.E., sir . . . *Very loud.* . . .'

They all felt the enemy passing very close down the starboard side. There was rushing, sluicing sound and *Seahorse* rocked crazily from side to side.

'Great God Almighty,' The Bodger whispered. 'The man's mad! Absolutely Harry starkers!'

'. . . Visitor lost in our own. . . .'

'Slow ahead together. Midships.'

' . . . Visitor faded. . . .'

There was a profound and thoughtful silence in the control room after the last sonar report. The Bodger became aware that the passageways on either side of the control room were crowded. He noticed the press of faces, all straining to see and hear what was happening.

The last exchange set the pattern for the next two hours. The Visitor circled *Seahorse* at a cautious distance before lunging inwards on a suicidal collision course. Again and again the ship's company clutched at pipes and brackets as the submarine rocked under the assaults. The Bodger was more than ever convinced that he was dealing with a submarine captain who had had a touch of the sun. However, crazy or not, the Visitor possessed a staggering underwater speed and manoeuvreability.

'He's making *rings* round us,' The Bodger said. 'But that's just about all he *is* doing. How long has the attack team been closed up?'

'Just under three hours, sir,' said Wilfred.

'Fall out the attack team. Keep the plot manned. The rest can fall out. Arrange the attack team in two watches.'

'Aye aye, sir.'

'Let me know whenever sonar picks him up again.'

As the hours passed, the Visitor's behaviour began to appear less unpredictable. His movements followed a definite sequence. He disappeared for one hour, circled for an hour and attacked at the end of the hour, only to disappear again. Just as The Bodger was hoping that he had gone for good, he came back. The Bodger came to anticipate the attacks and stood by the officer of the watch as the Visitor hurtled past. The rest of the time The Bodger sat in the wardroom and waited, like a billiard player sweating it out while his opponent ran up a huge break.

At supper time, Dangerous Dan was sitting in the wardroom looking very thoughtful.

'I wonder if I might make a suggestion, Bodger?'

'Of course.'

'I've been thinking about that black box of mine. I believe I can fix it to read up to about a thousand feet below us. I can cut out the response from the sea bottom by altering the scale. It won't be very accurate but it might give you a line on him. . . .'

'What a splendid idea, Dan!'

'It'll only be any use while he's below us, of course. . . .'

'That doesn't matter. It's better than nothing. Can you start it now?'

'Surely.'

'He's not due back for another half an hour. Will that give you time?'

'Ample. It's all calibrated and warmed up anyway.'

'Splendid! What a brilliant idea, Dan!'

Dangerous Dan shrugged modestly. 'All done by kindness,' he said.

Dangerous Dan climbed down again to his apparatus. Soon, it was clear that something was wrong with the black box. Dangerous Dan passed to and fro, a worried frown on his face.

'Something wrong, Dan?'

'I don't know. There doesn't *seem* to be anything wrong but I can't get any sense out of the thing at all. Something's jamming it. It won't read anything beyond about fifty feet below us.'

'Perhaps it didn't like having the scale altered?'

'No, that shouldn't affect it. I do it every day when I'm calibrating it anyway. But it just won't read beyond fifty feet now.'

'Perhaps. . . .'

Dangerous Dan started back towards the Coxswain's store, stopped, and clapped a hand to his forehead.

'I've got it! How stupid of me! Of *course* there's nothing the matter with it! It's telling us what we want to know.'

'What do you mean?'

'That's where our friend is.'

'I still don't get it.'

'That's where our little Visitor is right now. He's gliding along. . . . Fifty feet beneath us. . . .'

The most profound silence of all settled over *Seahorse*. The Bodger ran his fingers through his hair. This was the end of the line. This was where the text-books stopped. The imaginations of those who compiled the Admiralty instructions on submarine tactics had never envisaged an enemy who shadowed his adversary fifty feet below him. The Bodger realised that he was now on his own.

'Let's stir it up! Warn all compartments to expect large angles.'

Using full speed, maximum angles and full wheel, The Bodger put *Seahorse* through a series of submarine aquabatics which would have made her designers' hair stand rigid. After each manœuvre The Bodger slowed down and listened. Leading Seaman Gorbles reported an empty sea. The black box screen was blank.

'That's foxed him,' The Bodger said with some satisfaction.

'. . . Visitor regained, one one zero, sir. . . .'

'*Damnation*! What's the battery now, Number One?'

'Last reading was thirty per cent left, sir,' said Wilfred.

'Take another one.'

The electricians' mates scrambled over the pilot cells with their hydrometers and took another reading of the density of the battery fluid.

'Twenty-five per cent, sir,' said Wilfred. 'On the drop. We had to borrow the Chief Stoker's hydrometer, sir. Ours wouldn't read low enough!'

'It looks as though we'll have to wrap this up very soon whether we like it or not,' The Bodger said. 'We've tried circus tricks. Now we'll try Grandmother's Footsteps. Can you put on a stop trim, Derek?'

'Yes, sir.'

'Carry on then. Mid, you'd better watch this if you want to learn about trimming.'

The Midshipman stood at Derek's shoulder while Derek approached the ultimate in trimming, the inner temple of the art. Using the classic method of putting wheel and planes amidships, Derek made a succession of minute adjustments to the trim, transferring only a few gallons at a time. Each time the hydroplanes resumed their functions, they appeared to have less and less to do, until Derek stopped the shafts and the submarine hung in the sea, motionless and level.

'Well done, Chief. Anything on sonar?'

'Negative, sir.'

'Anything on the black box, Dan?'

'Nothing Bodger.'

'*That'll* give him something to think about,' said The Bodger.

The words had hardly left his lips when The Bodger felt *Seahorse's* deck tilt, and slowly right itself again. Just as The Bodger had convinced himself that his sense of balance was playing tricks on him, the deck slowly tilted again. The Bodger felt the hair prickle on his scalp.

'Full astern together! Sorry about your trim, Chief....'

The Bodger's order had an immediate and dramatic effect. *Seahorse* heeled violently. Dangerous Dan's black box blew all its fuses. Leading Seaman Gorbles gained contact at once and reeled off a string of bearings.

As the bearings were being plotted, The Bodger noticed that for the first time since the attack began the Visitor's change of bearing suggested a steady course and speed.

'Stand by for a firing set-up! Slow ahead together. Bring all after tubes to the action state. Chop chop with the tubes!'

The Bodger's best estimate of the Visitor's course and speed was set up by the attack team. The firing bearing was computed. The tubes were reported in the action state. Wilfred gripped the handle which would release the first torpedo. The Bodger raised his stop watch.

'Stand by . . . Stand . . . by. . . .'

At the last moment, when The Bodger's lips were actually framed to give the order to fire, the possible consequences of what he was about to do smote him. *Seahorse's* action might be the crossing of the Rubicon. The torpedo they were about to fire might have the same effect upon the world as the first shot fired at Sarajevo. The Bodger hesitated, but did not dare to give the order to break off. He did not dare to make any sound whatever. The long weeks of training, the weary attack team drills, had led to this moment. At this stage of the attack there could now be no other order than that to fire. If The Bodger so much as coughed, if he did no more than clear his throat, Wilfred would fire.

The Bodger waited while the perspiration gathered in his eyebrows and trickled into his eyes, not even daring to raise his hand to wipe it away. The seconds passed, the firing bearing was reached and overshot. Still The Bodger made no movement nor sound. At last, after a minute, the attack team relaxed. It was obvious that the Captain had changed his mind.

The Bodger swallowed. 'Do not fire,' he said hoarsely.

'. . . Visitor surfaced, sir!'

'Are you certain?'

'Positive, sir,' said Leading Seaman Gorbles, scornfully. Think I don't know when a bloody target's surfaced? he said to himself.

'Right. Any other H.E.?'

'Negative, sir.'

'Sixty feet. Stand by to surface. Diving stations.'

As *Seahorse* rose to periscope depth, The Bodger ordered all the control room lighting switched on. The submarine had been dived for more than twenty hours and he had no wish to be blinded by the daylight.

At sixty feet, The Bodger swung the periscope, tensed to go deep again. When he reached a bearing on the port bow, Wilfred was interested to see a deep blush rise from The Bodger's neck to his forehead.

'Surface.'

The Bodger followed Rusty and the Signalman up to the bridge. It was another beautiful day, with a calm sea and a bright sun.

But The Bodger was not interested in the weather. He searched the sea through his binoculars.

'There's our Visitor,' he said, pointing.

Two miles off the port bow, a very large grey whale was disporting itself in the sea. As The Bodger watched, it sounded but, before it disappeared, The Bodger swore he saw one huge mammalian eye close in a wink.

Feeling like an old man, The Bodger pressed the button of the bridge action speaker.

'Wireless Office, this is the Captain. Make to Captain S/M: Have broken off navel engagement with amorous whale.'

The Signalman's lip curled. 'You sex mad *monster*,' he said bitterly.

12

The episode of the Amorous Whale was not mentioned in *Seahorse* again. Nobody on board wished to be reminded of a time when they had all been braced at action stations to fight off the erotic advances of an affectionate marine mammal. Even Dangerous Dan, who could have dined out for months on it, expunged the story from his conversation, realising that true friendship often demands a true sacrifice. When Captain S/M examined *Seahorse's* log at the end of the quarter and remarked on the day and the night during which H.M.S. *Seahorse* appeared to have been at war, The Bodger shrugged it off, saying that he thought the ship's company had been getting stale and it seemed a good opportunity to liven them up a bit. But privately, in his own wardroom, The Bodger looked back on the episode in a mood of self-reproach.

'I was so *obsessed* by the idea that it was another submarine, when the damned animal was doing everything but *tell* us he was only trying to be friendly. He even came up and nuzzled our ship's side. When I think that I was within an ace of firing ... That would have been the most jilted whale this side of the Gosport ferry! But I suppose there's a moral to be drawn from it. We live in such suspicious times that we're apt to fly off the handle for anything. We're like people who're so scared of burglars we shoot the milkman dead.'

After the Whale, Dangerous Dan's experiments seemed an anti-climax. Even the Black Box lost its appeal and everyone was glad when the experiments were completed and *Seahorse* headed towards South America.

The nearest representative of the Royal Navy was H.M.S. *Beaufortshire*, flying the flag of the Commodore Amazon & River Plate Estuaries who was on his way to pay an official visit to the Republic of SanGuana d'Annuncion. The Bodger received a signal ordering him to proceed to Cajalcocamara, the capital of the Republic, for fuel, water and mail.

'Cajalcocamara,' said The Bodger thoughtfully, when he read the signal. 'That rings a bell.'

'What's it like, sir?'

'Bloody good run ashore. We quelled a revolution there once, when I was in the Cadet Training Cruiser.'

'SanGuana? That rings a bell with me too,' said Dangerous Dan. 'If I remember rightly, they have a very big motor race there at this time of the year. Let me look in my diary.'

Dangerous Dan took out a handsome green leather diary and opened it on the wardroom table. As Dangerous Dan thumbed through the pages, Dagwood could not help noticing that every day in Dangerous Dan's year seemed to be marked by a prominent social or sporting occasion, from the Cheltenham Gold Cup through The Trooping of The Colour to the Chelsea Arts Ball, by way of the Braemar Gathering.

'Here we are. The International Targa Mango da SanGuana. It's one of the big races of the year. It counts towards the World Racing Driver's Championship.'

'When is it?' Derek asked.

'Next Sunday.'

'When are we due to get there, Gavin?'

'Friday morning. That's if your donks don't give any trouble.'

'Don't worry,' said Derek. 'They won't if there's any danger of me missing the race. I'll speak to them kindly.'

'Taking it by and large, it should be a good time to visit the place,' The Bodger said.

It was an excellent time to visit Cajalcocamara. The city was already decorated for carnival in honour of the motor race, and the visit of two warships completed the San-Guana's celebrations. The citizens of the young Republic had not forgotten the part the Navy had played in winning them their independence. As *Seahorse* approached her berth she was played in by two brass bands and a native SanGuana orchestra playing on reeds and gourds. The dock buildings were decked with flags and the jetty was a packed mass of beaming faces. On the jetty's edge stood a welcoming committee of the city's most important citizens, including the President of the Republic, Aquila Monterruez himself, his cabinet, the British Consul, the Mayor, the Gieves Representative, the Principal of SanGuana University, the Man from the Prudential and the sporting editor of *The SanGuana*, the official organ of the Republican party.

'I don't see any sign of *Beaufortshire*?' said The Bodger. 'Golly, we've certainly got the first eleven out to meet us. Who would you say that little man in the yachting cap was?'

'The Admiralty Representative, sir,' said Wilfred.

'My God, I expect you're right!'

The Bodger marvelled, as he had marvelled many times in the past, at the wideness of the Admiralty's net.

'I bet if you paddled a canoe right up the bloody Amazon you'd find a little man from the Admiralty at the top waiting to come on board and tell you you'd already used up your year's allocation of parrots!'

The Bodger barely had time to get down to the casing before Aquila Monterruez was on board.

'My dear Bodger!' he cried, advancing with hand outstretched. 'How very refreshing to see you again! But how are you?'

'Very well indeed, Beaky,' said The Bodger. 'And you?'

'*Thriving*, me dear fellow! Do you know, this is the first time I have *ever* been on board one of these inventions. Perhaps I'd better make the introductions. I won't introduce my cabinet, they're a very mundane lot. The British Consul, though. . . .'

The British Consul shook hands stiffly. He felt that his position had been usurped by the ebullient Aquila. He was a tall man with weary blue eyes and shaggy eyebrows. He reminded The Bodger of one of those indolent baboons at the zoo which lean up against the bars of their cages and ignore the passing public.

'And this little man who looks as though he's carrying a heavy weight about on his head is one of yours, Bodger. The Admiralty Rep.'

Absent-mindedly patting the Admiralty Rep. on the head as he passed, Aquila followed Wilfred down to the wardroom.

'Very cosy,' he said when he saw it. The Bodger introduced his officers and Dangerous Dan. 'Very cosy indeed. Is there room for a bar?'

Wilfred hesitated, but The Bodger nodded. It was a quarter past nine in the morning but The Bodger was not one to deny hospitality to a President in his own country. Besides, now that he came to think of it, a drink would go down very well indeed. The Midshipman poured out gins and tonics all round except for the Admiralty Representative who asked for whisky and said unexpectedly: 'Salud y pesetas y fors en las brigitas!'

'Hear hear,' said Aquila.

The Signalman, who was also the ship's postman, appeared at the wardroom door.

'Mail, sir,' he said shortly. He passed The Bodger a bundle of private and official correspondence.

'Hullo?' The Bodger examined one letter. 'A letter for the Midshipman postmarked Oozemouth! What's all this, Mid?'

The Midshipman blushed delicately. 'There's a girl there who writes to me occasionally, sir,' he said.

'Voi che sapete, che cosa e amor?' hummed Dagwood.

'. . . And one for Pilot with a pink envelope and . . .' The Bodger sniffed. 'Perfume! You'll be making the Steward jealous, Pilot.'

'Her letters are a lot more attractive than she is, sir,' said Gavin.

'Come, lad,' said The Bodger, sternly. 'Think of the lovin' 'ands wot penned this 'ere missive. A man hasn't grown up until he's been embarrassed by a few love letters.'

The Signalman reappeared. 'Santa Claus has remembered you, sir,' he said to Derek.

'Has he?'

'Bloody great package on the casing, sir. They're trying to get it through the fore hatch now.'

Aquila clapped his hands. 'I'm dying to see what this is! It came a fortnight ago in the diplomatic bag and it's been hanging around the British Consulate ever since.'

'How did you know that?' The British Consul inquired sourly.

'My dear Fruity, you're so naïve only the British would employ you. I've been keeping my Chief of Police, a crude man, off it ever since it arrived. He swore it was a time bomb but I reassured him. I told him that the British, like the Americans, only send time bombs to their friends. But open it Derek, do. I'm all agog!'

Just then the Chief Stoker and his store-keeper Ferguson staggered past the wardroom, bent under the weight of a large black wooden packing case. As he passed, the Chief Stoker directed at Derek a glance of such concentrated hatred that Derek hastily finished his drink and hurried out to the control room.

The packing case seemed to fill a good part of the control room. It lay between the periscopes, already surrounded by a crowd of curious sailors.

'What have we got here, Chief Stoker?' Derek asked cheerily and, in the opinion of the Chief Stoker, stupidly.

'Don't know, sir.'

'It's a spare Chief Stoker!' called Able Seaman Ripper.

'We already got one spare——,' replied another, anonymous, voice.

'Quiet there,' the Chief Stoker growled. 'Got that crowbar?'

The top planks were prised off, uncovering strips of foam rubber which themselves enclosed another metal box with a screwed lid.

'Got a screw-driver?'

The lid was unscrewed and a further box wrapped in oiled paper appeared. The Chief Stoker set to work with the crowbar again.

'It's getting smaller and smaller, anyway,' Derek said.

The Chief Stoker grunted and wrenched off the lid. A

mass of straw spilled over the deck. Parting the straw, the
Chief Stoker lifted out a brown paper parcel the size of a
shoe box bound with transparent adhesive tape.

'Got a knife?'

Able Seaman Ripper produced a knife. The Chief
Stoker slit the tape and, like a conjurer, produced a small
cardboard box.

'Abracadabra.'

'You'd better open this, sir.'

Derek opened the box and took out a small brass gauge
with a round dial six inches in diameter. It was a combined
pressure and vacuum gauge of the kind used on submarine distillers.

'Was it a time bomb?' Aquila asked.

'No,' Derek said brusquely. 'It was what is known as
Preservation, Identification and Packing.'

The rest of the mail was by comparison undistinguished.
All the wardroom received tailors' bills which were all
thrown into the waste-paper basket.

'Have another drink, Beaky,' said The Bodger.

'Thank you, Bodger. Talking of tailors' bills. . . .'

'I remember getting a rude letter from my tailors when
I was at Oxford,' said the Admiralty Representative,
again unexpectedly: 'I settled them quite simply. I told
them that it was my custom to put all my outstanding
bills in a hat at the end of the month, draw one out, and
pay it. I told them that if I got another letter like that
theirs wouldn't even go into the hat!'

At that moment it occurred to Derek that if he wanted
a good view of the motor race, Aquila was just the fellow
to ask.

'How's your glass, sir? Let me get you another.'

'What a very christian idea, my dear Derek!'

'I hear you have a big motor race on Sunday, sir?'

'Indeed yes. The International Targa Mango da SanGuana. Rather a pretentious, pompous name I've always thought but the press like it. It looks so well on paper. Rolls off the tongue, too. You must all come as my guests, I won't accept any refusal. My Chief of Police, though a very obtuse man in many ways, will arrange seats for you.'

'Thank you *very* much, sir!' cried the wardroom in chorus.

'A pleasure. I shall be there myself of course, for political reasons. But I'd just as soon not. The *noise*, and all those impossible *people*! Some of them seem to think that just because they can drive one of those beastly machines at more than a hundred miles an hour I should offer them my own bed and toothbrush! It's too much. I had a go myself one year and some ill-mannered boor rammed into the back of me before I had gone three hundred yards, to say nothing of three hundred miles.'

'Can anyone drive then, sir?' Dangerous Dan asked. The Bodger looked suspicious; for a moment he thought he had recognised an undertone in Dangerous Dan's voice which reminded him of the past.

'Of course,' said Aquila. 'The race used to be open to all comers but the whole thing has grown so much that everyone except the big boys have been squeezed out. I'm told the race is now as important as Le Mans or the Mille Miglia, whatever they may be. There was a rather trying argument one year because the slower drivers were supposed to be getting in the way of the faster ones. I couldn't understand what they were arguing about myself. The whole *thing* seemed equally fraught with peril to me. Anyhow, I stopped it. But there's no reason why I shouldn't start it again. After all, I *am* President.

It's *my* race. Why,' Aquila said, draining his glass, 'do you want a drive?'

'*Would* I?' Driving in a motor race of such magnitude would be, in Dangerous Dan's eyes, second only to opening for England in the Lords Test.

'How's your glass, sir?' Derek said.

'My dear hospitable Derek. . . .' Aquila relinquished his glass.

'Really Monterruez,' protested the British Consul. 'You're not seriously suggesting. . . .'

'Consul,' said Aquila solemnly. He had had just enough alcohol to make him argumentative. 'You are forgetting that our host, Commander Badger here, received the Freedom of Cajalcocamara for his valiant part in my revolution. To a Freeman of Cajalcocamara, all things are possible! How about it, Bodger?'

The Bodger caught the British Consul's eye.

'No really, Beaky, it's very kind of you but I'm afraid I must refuse.'

'I'm disappointed in you, Bodger.'

The shape of the Second Coxswain loomed in the passageway.

'*Beaufortshire* just entering harbour, sir.'

'Dear God, that dreadful man,' Aquila said wearily. 'He visited me last year and bored me almost into an asylum. Do you know that sensation as though someone were drilling steadily into the top of your head? That describes it exactly. He reminds me sometimes of Chief of Police. He has the same inability to think of more than one thing at a time.'

'Who's that?'

'Commodore Richard Gilpin.'

'Is *he* here?' said The Bodger hoarsely.

'He's Commodore Amazon and River Plate and how's

your father. But I must go. Let *him* call on *us*. Come on Fruity,' Aquila nudged the British Consul, 'down with that one. We must be off.'

As he stepped out into the passageway, Aquila collided with an agitated Petty Officer Telegraphist.

'Signal from *Beaufortshire* sir: You are in my berth!'

'Nonsense,' said Aquila sharply. 'A Freeman of Cajalcocamara can berth anywhere he likes. Just you send him this message. . . .'

'That's all right, Beaky,' The Bodger intervened hastily. 'We've got to shift berth anyway. He's going to give us some fuel.'

'Oh, very well.'

Aquila marched across the gangway to his little car, pushed the British Consul into the passenger's seat, and prepared to drive off. He appeared to have some difficulty in finding the starter but at last the engine fired, the car backed and filled for a time, and then moved off in low gear.

Meanwhile, The Bodger was manœuvring *Seahorse* away from the jetty and out of *Beaufortshire's* way. He was only just in time. *Beaufortshire's* bows slid in behind *Seahorse's* stern as The Bodger backed out.

'What a rude man,' said The Bodger quietly.

Seahorse lay off while *Beaufortshire* secured in a flurry of bugle calls, band music and arms drill.

'*Beaufortshire's* flashing us, sir.'

'So I see. What's he saying, Signalman?'

'You—May—Salute—My—Flag—At—Noon, sir.'

The Bodger blinked. 'Has he gone mad? What does he think I'm running here, a Royal Naval Barracks?'

'It's five minutes to twelve now, sir.'

'I know.'

The Bodger had already been nettled by *Beaufortshire's*

signals. He was well aware that his own ship, with rusty sides and gaps in the casing where plates had been torn bodily away by the sea, compared poorly with *Beaufortshire's* spotless paintwork. He had been goaded almost beyond endurance by *Beaufortshire's* white uniforms and bugle calls, a display of ceremonial which he had hoped to avoid for his own ship's company who were weary after a long sea passage. But the order to fire a gun salute was too much. The last bond of restraint snapped in The Bodger's mind.

'How many guns does a Commodore get?'

'Eleven, sir,' said Wilfred.

'Pass the message to the Torpedo Officer to go up to the fore ends and fire eleven white smoke candles from the forrard underwater gun! At the double!'

On the stroke of noon, the first canister curved into the air and dropped into the harbour. A massive plume of white smoke billowed from it. The Torpedo Instructor stood in the fore ends, taking his time from Rusty, and chanting: 'If I wasn't a T.I., I wouldn't be here. . . .'

When the salute was finished, Cajalcocamara harbour was enveloped in a dense smoke cloud and a foul smell of carbide.

'From *Beaufortshire*, sir: Are you on fire?'

'Make to *Beaufortshire*: Only with enthusiasm. Intend coming alongside you now.'

Seahorse felt her way cautiously alongside *Beaufortshire*, The Bodger sounding the fog-siren in a most ostentatious manner.

Seahorse's officers were invited to take lunch in *Beaufortshire*. The meeting between the two wardrooms did not prosper. *Beaufortshire* had a social wardroom. As a mess, they were the last remaining stanchions of a way of life which vanished from the Royal Navy on September 3rd, 1939. They had a reputation as the most ferocious pride of social lions on either side of South America. The Amazon & River Plate Station might have been designed for their benefit. They rarely met another warship and bore the whole weight of the Navy's official entertaining on both sides of the continent, a burden under which any other wardroom would have collapsed. *Beaufortshire's* Navigating Officer explained the rigours of the commission to Gavin.

'Didn't get any sleep for three nights running in Rio. And B.A. was beyond a joke. The races were on and people literally queued up to take us out, old boy. We were almost glad to get back to sea for a rest. I expect you find the same?'

'Not exactly.'

'Where have you just come from?'

'Portsmouth.'

'Take you long?'

'Forty-one days.'

Dagwood and Rusty were being entertained by the Captain of Royal Marines.

'I expect the first things you chaps'll want is a bath, eh? Wash some of the smell off. Pretty smelly things, submarines, I'm told, eh?'

'Oh not at all,' said Dagwood. 'All submarines have baths let into the deck. Black marble ones.'

'You're pulling my leg! Black marble! What's that for?'

'Night vision,' Dagwood said seriously.

'Great Scott! I never thought of that! I suppose you have to worry about that sort of thing in submarines, eh?'

'I should say so. Their Lordships are always telling us

we must take more care over our sailors' health. We get vitamin tablets, extra orange juice, sun-ray lamps, what else, Rusty?'

'Masseur,' said Rusty, right on cue.

'Oh yes. Masseurs. And pornography.'

'*Pornography!*'

'Oh yes, specially issued to submarines,' Dagwood looked carefully at the Captain of Royal Marines. Reassured, he went on. 'They come in plain wrappers as a special supplement to the Advancement Regulations. People work up quite a frustration in submarines, you know. It's all that sea time.'

'I can understand that! Have another drink, eh?'

'Thank you,' said the frustrated Dagwood. 'I will.'

Derek was conducting the ritual negotiations between Engineer Officers concerning matters of fuel, lubricating oil and technical assistance. *Beaufortshire's* Engineer Officer was a fat florid Lieutenant Commander with a hearty laugh and a firm disinclination to be troubled by details.

'How much fuel can you let us have, sir?'

'See my Chief Stoker. He'll fix you up.'

'Is it Admiralty fuel?'

'Haven't the faintest idea, dear old chap! Shouldn't think so, for a moment. A little black man came on board somewhere along the coast, forget where it was now, and flogged us some.'

'But how about water content and all that?'

'Haven't the *faintest* idea. I expect my Chief Stoker puts a line down and if he catches a fish he knows there's water about, ha ha!'

'Yes,' said Derek.

Wilfred was also conducting a tribal pow-wow with *Beaufortshire's* First Lieutenant on such esoteric matters as showers for the ship's company, canteen opening hours, fresh bread, and dress for libertymen. He was finding the going as hard as Derek.

'How about mail, sir? Will your postman collect ours with yours?'

'Tell you what. Why don't you ask your Coxswain to see my Coxswain and let them sort it out for themselves? Do you shoot? We got some very good duck at Recife. We might have a day here, if you're interested.'

'I'm afraid I haven't done any for a long time.'

'How about you, sir?' *Beaufortshire's* First Lieutenant turned on Dangerous Dan who was staring, with bare-faced horror, at a coloured print of the M.F.H. of the West Rutland Hunt of 1843 which was hanging above the wardroom fireplace.

'I beg your pardon?'

'I said, do you shoot?'

'All our shoots are let.'

The First Lieutenant registered immediate interest.

'I didn't catch your name, sir . . . ?'

'Sudbury-Dunne. S.U.D.B . . .'

'Ah, your mother was a Pye-Gillespie before she married, wasn't she?'

'Correct.'

'I believe I had a day at your place once.'

'I doubt it. Unless you know the Prime Minister well? Perhaps you do.'

In the Commodore's day-cabin, The Bodger himself was having as sticky a time as his wardroom.

'Good to see you again, Badger,' Richard Gilpin was saying, coldly.

The Bodger, sitting on the edge of his chair nursing a

glass of South African sherry, permitted himself a non-committal grunt.

'We last met when you were my Number One in *Carousel*, is that right?'

'Yes, sir.'

'Fine ship. Fine ship. Fine wardroom. Fine ship's company.'

'Yes, sir.'

Inwardly, The Bodger marvelled at the way Richard Gilpin could contrive to look more like a naval officer than it seemed possible, or permissible, a naval officer should. Standing there by the fender, pouring himself a glass of sherry, his white uniform contrasting pleasantly with his lean tanned face, framed between the portrait of Nelson and the photograph of Admiralty Arch, Richard Gilpin might have been posing for a gin advertisment.

'I noticed several of your ship's company needed haircuts this morning, Badger.'

'They've been at sea a month, sir.'

'Yes.' Richard Gilpin took a seamanlike sip at his sherry. 'What was all that smoke this morning as we came in?'

'We had a little trouble with the forrard underwater gun, sir.'

'Yes, I suppose we must make allowances for the . . .' Richard Gilpin paused, '. . . illegitimate branches of the service.'

When The Bodger reached the safety of *Seahorse's* wardroom again, he said: 'Mid. Go ashore now. Find Aquila Monterruez. Tell him, from me, I would be delighted to accept his offer to drive in his motor race!'

The wardroom gave a concerted cheer. Dangerous Dan looked like a pilgrim granted a glimpse of Mecca.

'By the way, sir,' said Wilfred. 'I'm afraid we've been asked to shift berth forrard of *Beaufortshire* as soon as we've completed fuelling.'

'Whatever for?'

The Midshipman went pink. 'It was my fault, sir. As we were coming into harbour this morning, Leading Seaman Gorbles said what a good idea it would be to show our films on the upper deck against *Beaufortshire's* ship's side, sir. So I'm afraid I jokingly asked their First Lieutenant if he would mind painting a white square on their side to give us a better picture. . . .'

'That does it! Mid, you can tell Aquila Monterruez that *Seahorse* will be entering a *team* for the International Targa Mango da SanGuana! Number One!'

'Sir!'

'Detail off a ship's motor racing team!'

'Aye aye, sir!'

Snorting with fury, The Bodger retired to his cabin with a bottle of whisky and a copy of the Highway Code.

13

The news that H.M.S. *Seahorse* was entering an equipe for
the Targa Mango was received by the British community
in Cajalcocamara with astonishment and delight. Once
they had assured themselves that the news was genuine,
the British community rallied round. Mr MacTavish,
the general manager of SanGuanOil, promised to supply
the team's petrol and oil; Mr MacIntosh, executive head
of SanGuana Motors (South America) Ltd promised
tyres, sparking plugs and accessories; while the Anglican
Church Ladies' Scooter Club provided crash helmets for
the whole team.

The problem of cars proved to be no problem at all.
The British community, except the British Consul, fell
over themselves to lend their cars until Scuderia *Seahorse*
(as they were christened by the SanGuana motoring
press) promised to be, if not the most practised, at least
the most varied, team in the race.

The British Consul was sternly against the project from
the start but when he saw the response from the rest of
the British community he felt obliged to show the way.
The Bodger was deeply moved when the British Consul,
Aaron-like, offered his own pearl-grey Armstrong-Siddeley.
It was an imposing model, with a bonnet as high as a

barn roof and doors which shut with a massive clang like the closing of a bank vault.

'Look after the old girl, won't you?' the British Consul said, wiping an unmanly tear from his eye.

The Bodger wrung the British Consul's hand wordlessly, recognising the magnificence of the gesture.

The planter who turned over his swamp-stained Land Rover to Gotobed and the Chef had a more earthy approach.

'I've filled the tank with petrol and the back with beer. All you've got to do now is get going and keep going. If you do that, you're sure to get a place. Only one in ten finish this race anyway.'

Mr MacLean, the managing director of the First National Bank of SanGuana and himself an experienced rally-driver, lent Wilfred and Derek his Sunbeam.

The car was a green saloon with the competent look of all veteran rally cars, being fitted with white-wall tyres, sunvisor, three spotlights, a row of motoring club badges and a large spade strapped to the boot.

On the morning of the race, The Bodger and his co-driver Dangerous Dan went down to have a look at the opposition. They could hear the noise from the square a mile away and if they had needed any convincing of the importance of the Targa Mango, the sight of the square itself provided it. The whole carnival of the international motor racing scene had been set up in the city of Cajalcocamara. Overhead banners advertised tyres, sparking plugs and brake linings. Girls in tight trousers and sunglasses, shoe-shine boys, lottery ticket sellers, tourists wearing coloured shirts and carrying cameras, short fat men in light tropical suits smoking cigars, and SanGuana policemen in khaki tunics and puttees paraded the square and inspected the cars. The cars were spaced out at intervals along the square and were surrounded by chattering groups of men in overalls, photographers and impatient men with badges in their buttonholes.

The Bodger and Dangerous Dan stopped by one gleaming red car. The engine was warming up with all the authority of high octane fuel, dual-choke carburettors, a trifurcated manifold, a dynamically-balanced crankshaft and twin overhead highlift camshafts. The driver, a dedicated-looking man called Danny Auber, was sitting in the driver's seat, nodding and holding up his thumb.

'Nice drop of motor car!' Dangerous Dan shouted.

The engine noise dropped. The Bodger kicked one of the superb high-hysteresis racing tyres. 'Cheap modern tin-ware,' he said.

Danny Auber, triple winner of the Nurburgring 1000 Kilometre, hoisted himself out of the bucket seat and approached them. He had heard all about The Bodger and his equipe.

'Do you mind? You may think this is *frightfully* funny. We don't. You see, we *work* here.'

The Bodger waved his hands deprecatingly. 'But my dear chap. Please don't mind us.'

Nonetheless, the Bodger was depressed by the incident. He felt like the captain of a visiting village cricket team who has arrived at the ground to find his side matched against the Australians.

'Which is just about what we are,' said The Bodger despondently.

The race was timed to start at noon but the first car away, Gotobed's Land Rover, mounted the starting ramp at eleven o'clock. This early start, unprecedented in the history of the race, was the outcome of a bitter argument between Aquila and the race officials. The race officials had protested vigorously against Scuderia *Seahorse's* entry. The race marshals had pointed to relevant definitions in the rule book. The time-keepers had quoted relevant passages in the minutes of meetings of bodies governing international motor racing. The scrutineers had appealed to Aquila's sense of honour. The pit managers had tried bribery.

Aquila remained adamant. Commander Badger was a Freeman of Cajalcocamara and, furthermore, was driving at the personal invitation of the President. Either Scuderia *Seahorse* went to the starting line or there would be no International Targa Mango da SanGuana. The race officials retired and, turning a corner, came suddenly upon the spectacle of Gotobed and the Chef, wearing very fetching lilac crash helmets, sitting in a battered Land Rover. The officials crossed themselves, returned to Aquila, and insisted that Gotobed and the Chef start an hour before the rest. Aquila could not refuse; he himself was secretly conscience-stricken by Gotobed's motor-racing aspect.

Gotobed and the Chef were given a combined send-off by the ship's companies of *Beaufortshire* and *Seahorse* and the citizens of Cajalcocamara which exceeded any ovation given any driver within living memory. The B.B.C. overseas commentator was so moved by the scene that he compared it to the historic occasion when the Flying Mantuan, the incomparable Nuovolari himself, won the race in an Alfa-Romeo at an average speed of sixty-eight miles an hour. (The Midshipman, who had been unanimously voted Duty Officer and was sitting disconsolately by himself in *Seahorse's* wardroom, was strangely cheered by this description and poured himself another very large whisky.)

The Bodger and Dangerous Dan drove on to the starting ramp at one minute to twelve. As the President's personal guest, The Bodger was given the honour of starting the race proper. The SanGuana press had already given him a volume of publicity normally reserved for visiting Presidents of the United States and the reception the crowd gave him reduced the radio commentator to weak repetitions of the word 'fabulous.'

As the great bell of the Church of the Immaculate Conception across the square tolled noon, amid the 'Vivas' of the crowd, and the ominous, predatory growling of the racing engines in the background, The Bodger and Dangerous Dan drove off.

The Targa Mango route lay first through the streets of Cajalcocamara and then out on to the eight-lane motorway which ran beside the sea to the Casino, twenty miles to the south, where the road turned sharply right and up into the mountains.

The motorway had been specially cleared of all other traffic. The lane lines extended to the horizon in a perfect example of perspective. It was not often that the Bodger was given a clear road and urged to drive as fast as he could along it. He pressed the accelerator to the floorboard and watched the speedometer climbing. He had settled in his seat and was beginning to enjoy himself when there was a banshee whine at his elbow, a blast of air and sound, and a low red car hurtled past and dwindled to a blur far ahead, its engine note rising and falling as the driver drew long sonorous chords from the close-ratio gearbox.

The Bodger was so startled that he almost lost control of his car. He had been shocked to discover that fast as he himself was driving he could be passed by another car travelling very much faster.

173

'He was still changing up, the bastard!' Dangerous Dan yelled in The Bodger's ear.

'Who was it?'

'Harry Boito! Broke the lap record three times running at the Nurburgring last year! Here comes another one! Don't bother about the mirror, Bodger! Just concentrate on driving! I'll tell you when he's coming. Here he comes *now. . . .*'

There was another roar and a blast of air and another car thunderbolted past them.

'Lew Cherubini! Won the Mille Miglia three years ago at an average of a hundred and five! They had to take his navigator Johnnie Dowland away afterwards!'

'Why?'

'He's been in a home ever since!'

The Bodger was driving at just over a hundred miles an hour but one by one the red, green, blue and silver cars overhauled him and went ahead to the Casino turn where they flicked out of sight. Dangerous Dan supplied biographical notes.

'. . . Ted Elgar and Gabby Faure! Only people who've ever won the Monte Carlo, the Tulip and the Safari in one year. . . .'

'. . . Charlie Gounod! Won the Indianapolis Five Hundred this year at an average of a hundred and forty. . . .'

'. . . Ferdy Herold! Just out of hospital! Turned over and caught fire at Monza two months ago. . . .'

Dangerous Dan's recital of the great names of motor racing lit a fierce fire in The Bodger's blood. He felt the competitive spirit rising in him. When he was overtaken yet again and forced out of line while approaching the Casino turn by a car which was travelling faster than any previous one, The Bodger swore and trod harder on the accelerator.

'. . . Let him *go*, Bodger! That was Jack Ibert! He's won this race twice running. . . .'

The other car slowed, drifted sideways, and accelerated out of the bend like a striking snake.

'Bodger,' Dangerous Dan said, in a small voice. 'Don't try and do it like that. . . .'

The mighty car heeled over. A group of SanGuanos standing by the straw bales leaped for their lives. Palm trees flickered across the bonnet. The wheel spun through The Bodger's hands. The road swung clear in front. The car came upright. Dangerous Dan opened his eyes again.

'Well done, Bodger,' he croaked, weakly.

Derek and Wilfred approached the Casino bend with superb confidence. Derek had once built himself a hot-rod special while he was at college and had competed in hill climbs and sprints. He was the only member of Scuderia *Seahorse* who had ever competed in any sort of motor race before and he swept Mr MacLean's Sunbeam round the bend like a veteran.

'That was neatly done, Derek,' said Wilfred.

'I wonder how far ahead the Boss is?'

'I shouldn't try and overtake him, if I were you.'

'Why not?'

'That would be the most tactless thing any engineer officer did to his C.O.!'

A mile behind, in the Admiralty Representative's black Mercedes, Rusty and Dagwood (Scuderia *Seahorse* were driving in Navy List order) approached the bend more circumspectly.

'Watch it, Rusty,' Dagwood cautioned. 'Don't let all this go to your head. This looks like a nasty one.'

'Don't worry, I always do cadence braking.'

'What's that for God's sake?'

'You put the brakes on and off until you get the front of the car bouncing. You pick up the natural frequency of the suspension and force the tyres harder on to the road. Derek told me about it.'

'All right, but just watch it.'

As it happened, Rusty was given the opportunity for only one cadence. At the first pressure of the brake pedal the front wheels entered an oil slick. Where Rusty should have swung right, the car slid onwards. Rusty cadence-braked off the track, through the spectators who scattered right and left, down in an elegant cadenza over a flight of steps and on to the Casino lawn where the car pivoted round and dived into a dense bank of hydrangeas. Dagwood's door flew open and he fell out in a praying position amongst the hydrangeas.

'All good things around us,' he sang in a hysterical voice, 'are sent from heaven above. . . .'

Rusty felt himself all over, got out of the car, walked back to the track and was just in time to see the Chief E.R.A. and the Outside Wrecker negotiating the Casino bend in the Gieves' Representative's red M.G. The Chief E.R.A. was hunched over the wheel, his brows knotted with concentration under his beige crash helmet. The Outside Wrecker, however, had lost his crash helmet and was leaning over the side of the car, retching. Recognising Rusty, he managed a despairing half-salute before he was whirled away.

Back at the starting ramp, the Coxswain and the Radio Electrician, two sombre individuals, were giving the race starters a deal of trouble. They had been lent the Chief of

Police's cerise and daffodil-coloured Cadillac hard-top and although the car was fitted with servo-assisted brakes, power-assisted steering and automatic two-pedal drive, the Coxswain was having difficulty in driving it up the ramp. At the third attempt the engine stalled.

The Coxswain pressed what he imagined was the starter button, whereupon the car underwent an extraordinary transformation. The wheels locked. Steel shutters rattled down over the windows. Steel blinds rose up to cover the doors. A red light blinked on the roof and a siren wailed on the front bumper. Inside the car, which was now an immobile steel box, articulated arms clamped steel helmets on the heads of the Coxswain and the Radio Electrician. Shutters on the dashboard slid back and revealed a brace of automatic pistols. In the opinion of the knowledgeable SanGuana crowd, it was even better than Gotobed.

There was a delay of several minutes before the Chief of Police's confidential locksmith was fetched from the crowd to free the wheels. The next two competitors, Connie Kreutzer and Leo Janacek, joint holders of the world land speed record for cars up to $1\frac{1}{2}$ litres, waited while the Coxswain and the Radio Electrician, still encased in their steel tomb, were wheeled away. Then, with a derisive exhaust blare and a shake of the fist, they were off.

Seahorse's next entrant was Gavin driving a plum-coloured Maserati, the property of Mr MacDonald, the principal of SanGuana University. He had as co-driver Miss MacDonald who was wearing a very chic pair of white overalls and a white crash helmet with an hibiscus blossom tucked under the rim. It looked as though Gavin was destined for an enjoyable Targa Mango and the crowd cheered him out of sight.

Gavin's place was taken by the Steward, sitting in a British racing green Jaguar lent by the manager of the Casino, a wealthy Levantine. The Casino manager had also lent his daughter, a striking ash-blonde who had been runner-up for the title of Miss SanGuana the previous year (the title being won by the daughter of the Chief of Police). At this point the B.B.C. commentator lost his voice and was thankful to be relieved by the shipping forecast.

After some fiddling with the radio, Dangerous Dan found a programme of opera excerpts. They reached the mountains and the Te Deum which ended Act One of *Tosca* together.

'Te aeternum Patreus omino terra veneratur!' Dangerous Dan chanted as The Bodger pulled the big car from side to side across the twisting road.

'How're we doing, Dan?'

Dangerous Dan looked at his watch. 'I make it we're averaging about fifty miles an hour. That's not nearly good enough for a win, of course, but it's not too bad.'

The Bodger's attention was caught by the driving mirror.

'Get back, you peasant,' he said.

Dangerous Dan glanced backwards. He had an impression of an infuriated steel animal with glass eyes surmounted by a pair of goggles, breathing down his neck.

'You'd better let them past, Bodger, or they'll burst something.'

'All right, but he'll have to wait until we reach a straight bit. I'm not going to stop on these bends. God, what a heavenly view!'

The trees had been cut back from each bend in the road and as the car turned they could see the coastline of SanGuana laid out below. Far away in the blue distance they could pick out the tiny buildings of the city and, on the seaward side, the dockyard and its toy ships.

'Here's a straight bit.'

'... That was Hank Litolff and Jud Meyerbeer! They're the last of the big boys. Did you notice the new rear suspension?'

'Not particularly.'

Higher in the mountains, Gotobed and the Chef were still leading the race by a considerable distance, being cheered through every village as they bowled along. They became so used to applause that they were surprised to reach one remote village where there was no cheering. The population was gathered round the only petrol pump in the village, silent, gloomy, as though they had gathered for the announcement of a catastrophe. A catastrophe had indeed occurred. The petrol pump was not working. It was the village's main industry; almost everybody made their livelihood, directly or indirectly, from the trade it brought. A mishap to the petrol pump was as great a disaster to them as the closing of the pit in a mining town. The village elders were congregated round the pump in solemn session. Now and then one of them tried the pump handle, with no success.

Gotobed stopped the Land Rover.

'Bliddy pomp's lost wackum,' he said.

The crowd parted to let him through. He examined the pump closely and then, taking up a large stone, began to batter the pump body with it. A rumble of anger passed among the villagers. Gotobed ignored them. He unscrewed a small cap on top of the pump and, placing his lips to the hole, blew.

There was a subterranean rumbling and a heavy odour of petrol. Gotobed replaced the cap and jerked the pump handle. With each jerk a jet of petrol spurted out into the road.

The villagers gasped as though they had been parties to a miracle and gave Gotobed a spontaneous round of applause. The elders took him in their arms and embraced him. The girls threw hibiscus blooms from their hair into the back of the Land Rover.

Blushing like a peony, Gotobed had his tank filled and drove off in a haze of petrol, hibiscus and good wishes.

Just outside the village, the road forked. The Targa Mango took the right-hand road, while the left-hand road led to the wildernesses of the interior, petering out in swamps and jungle. The village elders put their heads together. One good turn deserved another. An adjustment was made to the road barriers.

The elders had just stepped back from the track when the first of Gotobed's pursuers appeared at the bottom of the village street, followed by the rest of the pack in full cry.

One after the other the shining, magnificent cars, the carriers of the flying horse, the three-pronged star and the raised trident, the bearers of the illustrious insignia and the famous initials, swept round to the left. Only Pete Mascagni and Karl Nicolai, fresh from their triumph at Le Mans and experienced Targa Mango drivers, attempted to bear right. The village elders imperiously waved them left.

When the procession of cars seemed to have stopped, the barriers were readjusted. The elders had hardly reached their places again when The Bodger appeared.

'Which way now, Dan?'

'Right.'

'Right.'

The next car was Gavin, who had been working steadily up through the field, bent on catching The Bodger. He had been driving above his skill and had already forced Leading Seaman Gorbles and the Signalman, in a pea-green Volkswagen provided by Mr MacGregor, the sporting editor of *The SanGuana*, into a ditch.

'In the old days,' Leading Seaman Gorbles remarked to the Signalman, as the sound of Gavin's engine died away, 'all the bastards were made dukes. Now all the bastards are made naval officers!'

But Gavin's retribution was near. Just as he caught sight of The Bodger, he misjudged the line of a bend and plunged off the road.

The car dropped bodily through some small trees, coasted down a slope and came to rest in a clearing between two bamboo clumps. A cloud of brilliant red butterflies rose into the air.

The trees rustled as they came upright again. An occasional engine droned along the road overhead, its sound filtered by the trees. The clearing looked out over the side of the mountain to the blue Pacific. The spot might have been chosen for a picnic, tête-à-tête.

Gavin turned and looked into the brown eyes, wide and startled as a fawn's. He kissed one shell-like ear under the hibiscus blossom.

'Darling,' he whispered. 'We've run out of road . . .'

14

Higher up on the mountain, on the next bend, The Bodger heard the sound of Gavin's passing.

'Sounds like one of our high-powered friends driving into the scenery.'

'Can't be,' Dangerous Dan said. 'They've all been practising for months for this race. They must be miles ahead by now. I'm afraid that must have been one of ours.'

'Well I can't stop now. Let's just hope the Next-of-Kin Book's up to date.'

They overtook Gotobed at the top of the mountain pass where he had stopped to admire the view and to start the second crate of beer. Here they changed drivers and Dangerous Dan took over for the hairpin descent down the mountainside, humming the chorus of the Grand March and Chorus from Act Two of *Aida* as he wrenched on the hand-brake to lock the rear wheels round the curves. The radio orchestra and chorus were bucking into the Soldier's Chorus from Act Four of *Faust* as Dangerous Dan drove out on the long dusty straights of the inland plateau.

'I wonder if the wind-screen washers work?' said Dangerous Dan.

The Bodger pressed a rubber bulb which might have

been borrowed from a Victorian dentist's surgery. Two jets of water struck the windscreen with the force of fire-hoses.

'Like opening an artery,' The Bodger said.

When the great bell of the Church of the Immaculate Conception struck half past four, a wave of alarm almost amounting to panic passed amongst the race officials at the finishing line. The winner of the Targa Mango could be expected to average just over seventy-five miles an hour and was due to finish any time after four and certainly before a quarter past. It was now after half past four and the five-mile Avenida d'Aquila, down which the winner must come, was still empty. Furthermore, it was plain from reports throughout the afternoon that strange things had been happening on the track. The true position was still not clear but officials at check-points along the route denied any knowledge of Joe Pergolesi, or Roger Quilter, or Jan Rameau or indeed any of the favourites. Every check-point relayed the same story. They had seen a pearl-grey Armstrong Siddeley, a green Sunbeam and a red M.G. but nothing else. Later, under pressure, they admitted to a Land Rover, driven fortissimo. But, emphatically, nothing else.

The finishing line control point was besieged by excited pit managers and reporters.

'What's happened to Alec Scriabin?'

'Do you mean to tell me they haven't seen *anything* of Joe Tartini? God, he's just won the Pan-American, he should take this one standing on his head!'

The officials wrung their hands, re-telephoned and returned with the same story, with the addition of a blue Vauxhall.

'That's my girl!' cried the Man from the Prudential. 'That's my car!'

'Who's driving that?'

The officials consulted the list.

'Señor C. Stoker and Señor S. Coxswain.'

'. . . And with that report from Arthur Sullivan, our correspondent in Cajalcocamara, we return listeners to the studio. . . .'

'Damn! I wish I'd got that station before. We might have got some idea of how we're doing, Dan.'

'We'll know in another half an hour. Can you get the opera again? I was rather enjoying that. Would you like to drive the last bit, Bodger?'

'That's very generous of you, Dan. I'd love to.'

It struck The Bodger that they had not seen another car for some time.

'You sure we're on the right road, Dan? We haven't seen another car for a fair old time.'

'We must be. They seem to be expecting us wherever we go. The Navy must be popularity boys round this neck of the woods, judging by the chuck-up we're getting. It's understandable, you know, Bodger. The bright boys can do a hundred and seventy on these stretches. They must be home and dry by now. Our team are all behind us. We're in between.'

'Between the sublime and the ridiculous,' said The Bodger.

Dangerous Dan looked at his watch. 'Still, we're not doing too badly. 'We're averaging a steady fifty. That's pretty good for beginners. If enough of the lunatics up front pile themselves into brick walls we might even get a place.'

The prospect of being placed in a major motor race went straight to The Bodger's head like old wine.

'Steady, old fruit,' said Dangerous Dan. 'I only said *might*. Ease off a bit. I've got a wife and two kids.'

Antonio Vivaldi, the man with the chequered flag, had once been a matador and he had brought his skill with the cape to the track. His cape-work now had more aficionados on the race track than it had ever had in the corrida. The greatest names in motor racing had flashed under his flowing veronicas. The Targa Mango was his favourite race. He had looked forward to it and had even practised a special pass in its honour. But, at five minutes to six, Antonio sadly decided that his services would not now, if ever, be required. Stuffing his flag into a hip-pocket, he retired to the staff cantina.

He had barely tipped the bottle to his lips when there came a great growling roar from the crowd outside. Antonio Vivaldi, of all people, did not need to be told the sound's significance. Such a cheer could only greet the first man home in the Targa Mango.

Spluttering and choking, Antonio Vivaldi was just in time to reach the finishing line, unfurl his flag, and wave it as The Bodger shot past. It was not a graceful movement and would have been hooted out of any bull-ring in Spain, but it was the best he could do with the wine still running down his chin. However, he recovered enough to execute a series of properly elegant passes over the unspeakable Sunbeam, the unmentionable M.G. and the indescribable Vauxhall which followed. Where the other drivers were, Antonio Vivaldi had no idea. He stuffed his flag away again and resumed his bottle, only vaguely conscious that he had played a walking-on part in the twilight of the gods.

There were no other finishers except, at midnight, an erratically-driven Land Rover and, at dawn, a Jaguar containing a dreamy Steward and a rapturous ash-blonde.

When the news of The Bodger's winning drive was first flashed round the world, incredulous editors searched their press cuttings and cabled their correspondents to come in out of the sun. It was not until a picture of The Bodger, garlanded, dust-stained, smiling, and being embraced by the Chief of Police's daughter, was radioed to the world's capitals and the headlines appeared 'British Cars, 1, 2, 3 in T. Mango!', 'New Racing Star!', and 'Gentlemen, A Toast—The Bodger!', that the motor racing press and industry awoke to the fact that they had been the victims of what *The Times* later described as 'the greatest turn-up for the book since David and Goliath.'

The three-legged donkey had won the Derby, slowing up. The tortoise had soundly thrashed the hare. Cartoonists hugged their sides and sharpened fresh pencils. In Modena and Turin and Coventry and Stuttgart men looked at each other in a wild surmise. In Detroit, executives fed the result into computers and said: 'Overseas-sales-wise, this is a severe reversalisation. It's gonna cost us several mega-bucks, R.J.' In Paris, small swarthy men tore their berets into shreds and jumped on them, crying: 'Nom d'un poisson, alors qu'est ce que c'est que ca, ce *Bodgaire*?' In London, a bewildered director of the winning firm was shaken from his club armchair and thumped on the back by the committee. All over the

United Kingdom, Chief Constables added another name to their lists.

Deep in the unmapped wilderness beyond the mountains of SanGuana, a long line of cars worth over a million pounds had come to a halt because the leading car was axle-deep in a swamp. The magnificent engines were now motionless, gently pinging as they cooled in the shade of a line of mango trees.

The wilderness had already begun the process of assimilation. Ants tentatively probed the superb high-hysteresis racing tyres and wandered questioningly over the mirror-finished engine surfaces. A large green snake dropped with a slithering plop into a bucket seat. The first tendril of a searching vine had completed half a careful revolution around the wire spoke of a wheel.

The drivers had left their cars and were clustered round Wolf-Ferrari who was studying a silver cigarette case on which was engraved a small-scale map of South America.

At half past one the next morning, The Bodger, still wearing his garland, walked back along the jetty towards *Seahorse* alone. The Bodger could not remember a time when he had been more pleased with himself and with life. He and Dangerous Dan had won the Targa Mango (although exactly how, The Bodger was still not sure). Aquila had been very hospitable. They had all been invited to a ball at the British Consulate where they had eaten Crème de Carburettor Soup, Lobster Thermidor au Armstrong Siddeley, Chicken M.G. with slices of orange Sunbeam, followed by café au Vauxhall. The wines had been excellent and plentiful. Afterwards The Bodger had danced with the Chief of Police's daughter who was South American rhumba champion. All sorts of genial people, and even Commodore Richard Gilpin, had come up and shaken him by the hand. He had refused an invitation to drive in the Dutch Grand Prix at Zandvoort the next week. Over the brandy Aquila had decided to form his own navy and offered him the job of Commander-in-Chief. Altogether it had been a memorable evening.

It had all been splendid, but shortly after midnight The Bodger had felt a need for solitude, a craving for that communion with his inner gods which comes upon many men after an evening's drinking. The Bodger's walk through the town led him, with that unerring instinct which leads a naval officer to his bunk like a homing pigeon, back to the jetty.

The Bodger steadied himself on *Beaufortshire's* gangway while he measured the remaining distance to *Seahorse* by eye. His attention was distracted by the row of lights hanging on the gangway rail. The lights fascinated him. They led his glance towards *Beaufortshire's* quarterdeck. It seemed to The Bodger an inviting sort of place.

Carefully, The Bodger mounted the gangway. The quartermaster at the top regarded him with hostility. The Bodger resented the man's look.

'Where's the Officer of the Day?'

'Turned in.'

'Well, get him out then.'

The Quartermaster hesitated. He had not yet placed The Bodger. He was definitely not one of *Beaufortshire's* officers but he had nevertheless an undefinable, familiar look about him.

'Tell him the Commanding Officer of H.M.S. *Seahorse* wants him.'

'Aye aye, sir.'

All the quartermaster's doubts were instantly resolved.

'Tell him I want the bar opened. Immediately. Urgently!'

Had the quartermaster then turned back and politely asked The Bodger to leave, all might still have been well. But the quartermaster only hesitated and went to call the Officer of the Day.

The Officer of the Day was the Navigating Officer.

'I'm afraid our bar is closed, sir,' he said coldly.

'*Closed!*' The Bodger pondered upon the enormity of the suggestion. 'What a ridiculous idea, if I may respectfully say so.'

'I'm sorry, sir.'

'Very well. Where's your captain?'

'The Captain is ashore, sir.'

There comes to every man at some time the sickening certainty that the bartender is not going to give him a drink. The Bodger bowed before the verdict.

'Very well.'

The Bodger negotiated the gangway once more. The quartermaster and the Navigating Officer congratulated themselves that they had conducted a tricky interview with tact and finesse, and retired.

With one foot on *Seahorse's* gangway, The Bodger stopped. An idea had just struck him. It was a concept of such imagination, such consummate daring, that The Bodger remained where he was for a moment, quite stunned by his own virtuosity.

Sober, The Bodger could contain his own more outrageous flights of humour; in the cold light of day, he could resist temptation. But under such a starlit night, after such a day, The Bodger resisted only briefly and capitulated.

The Bodger looked cautiously over *Beaufortshire's* upper deck. It was deserted. Stealthily he moved along the jetty, removed *Beaufortshire's* wires from the bollards, and placed them on the jetty. Then he ran to *Seahorse*, crossed the gangway, saluted gravely, and mounted to his own bridge.

'Slow ahead together,' he said.

Like a cat The Bodger shinned down the ladders and padded aft to the motor room where he again saluted and said: 'Slow ahead together, sir, aye aye, sir.'

The Bodger made the switches and set the submarine's main motors turning slowly ahead.

'Both main motors going ahead, sir,' he said, in a reasonable imitation of the Signalman's sepulchral voice.

The Bodger ascended to the bridge and said to the voice-pipe: 'Very good.'

He remained for some time looking aft, watching the water churning from *Seahorse* towards *Beaufortshire*.

'Stop together.'

Once more, The Bodger descended to the motor room.

'Stop together, sir. Aye aye, sir.'

The Bodger broke the main motor switches, walked forward to his cabin, and stretched himself, still fully clothed and garlanded, upon his bunk.

In the distance, as he fell asleep, The Bodger could hear the sound of voices but they were no more to him than the faraway buzzing of flies around a rubbish heap on a hot summer's day.

15

A submarine returning from abroad was normally given a very modest press reception—seldom more than a column and a photograph in the local paper and a paragraph in the national press. H.M.S. *Seahorse's* return from San-Guana was given the most complete press coverage the Submarine Service had ever experienced. A helicopter met the ship in the Channel, before she had raised St Catherine's, before even Geronwyn Evans had struck his tuning fork and led off 'First the Nab and then the Warner.' She was photographed every inch of the way to her berth where Captain S/M and his staff were fighting to keep their feet amongst the television cameras and the clamouring crowd of reporters and families. Photographers swarmed over the jetty and the catamarans, snapping *Seahorse's* ensign, The Bodger's hat, Leading Seaman Gorbles, and in passing, the Naval Correspondent of the *Daily Disaster* who was struck smartly on the head by *Seahorse's* first heaving line.

Some of the press deployed to interview members of the Ship's Company but most of them made for The Bodger. The Bodger was ready for them.

'It was team-work that did it,' he said, solemnly. 'Team-work all the way.'

'Commander Badger,' said the Naval Correspondent of the *Daily Disaster*, 'do you intend to take up motor racing seriously? Don't misunderstand me, I mean you've won the Targa Mango but. . . .'

'I don't intend to race again.'

'Commander Badger, is it true that you drove in this race as publicity for the Royal Navy?'

The Bodger thought very hard, very swiftly; this question had a curly, spiked tail.

'My team and I drove at the personal invitation of the President, as his guests.'

'Commander Badger,' said the editor of *Woman and Garden* coyly, 'there's a rumour of a romance between you and Señorita Alvarez. . . .'

'Who's she?'

'Come, come, Commander. The daughter of the Chief of Police.'

'Oh *her!*' A delighted smile spread over The Bodger's face. This was a moment for which he had waited all his adult life.

'No,' he said slowly, 'we are just good friends.'

Whatever the reaction in the national press, The Bodger's return was only a one day sensation in the Submarine Service. The Submarine Service had more important things to think about. The Reunion was due.

The Reunion was the submariners' annual beano. Its date was sacred in every submariner's diary; only death took precedence (and then only after the Mess Secretary had been informed). The Reunion had the same effect on submariners as the Bonnie Prince's fiery cross had upon the clansmen. For it, they abandoned their wives and families. They left their desks at Lloyds, their farms in Dorset, their market gardens in Leicestershire, their bookshops in Winchester, and their garages in Croydon. They left their offices, their sales rooms, their boards, their spades, their benches, their psychologists' couches and converged upon Portsmouth like a mass migration of thirst-crazed lemmings. The first of them began to assemble three days before the event and the last of them were not normally carried away until three days after it and while the Reunion was in progress the foreign exchange market could collapse in ruins, the Middle East flame in insurrection, earthquakes devastate the western hemisphere and the whole of England itself submerge under a tidal wave but all those who had ever been submariners would remain oblivious, gathered under one roof and pouring whisky down their assembled throats just as fast as it would drain away.

When they were all present, the submariners could claim at least one holder of almost every honour, medal and decoration in the Gazette. There were men at the Reunion who had fought a submarine through the nets and mine cables of the Dardanelles into the Sea of Marmara and watched a Turkish cruiser settle on the bottom. There were men there who had patrolled in a submarine in the shallow water, the sudden freshwater layers, and the short summer nights of the Skagerrak. There were men who had run blind through the minefields of the Java Sea with a magnetic compass, a stop-watch and several prayers. There were men who had been depth-charged constantly for a day and a half, who had heard a mine-cable scrape the length of the ship before swinging clear, who had swum seven miles to shore after their ship was mined, who had cleared unexploded bombs from the casing in broad daylight, and who had escaped from three hundred feet with buckets over their heads. They represented a weapon which, in its British guise, had borne the heat and burden of the war from the Atlantic to the Pacific by way of the Mediterranean, and which, in its American counterpart, had crippled the Japanese navy and ripped the bottom out of the Japanese mercantile fleet. It was also a weapon which, used by the enemy, had brought the United Kingdom itself within a few months of starvation.

'All I can say is,' said Dangerous Dan, who was already on his fourth whisky, 'you wouldn't think it to look at them.'

Dangerous Dan had often noticed that the most distinguished submarine officers were also the scruffiest. 'There's normally a fly-button missing for every D.S.O.,' he said.

Dangerous Dan's eye rested on the Senior Submariner present, a venerable and very distinguished Admiral whose uniform was encrusted with orders and who possessed a row of medals fourteen inches in length and forty years in time. The Senior Submariner was now wearing a very baggy and faded Glen check with scuffed leather elbow-pieces.

'As I see it,' the Senior Submariner was saying to a circle of clients, 'submarines haven't advanced a bit since I joined 'em. Not one bit!'

The circle of clients clicked their teeth deprecatingly.

'*You* sir,' the Senior Submariner said to a very young, fair-haired submarine C.O. with brilliant white teeth who had just taken over his first command. 'What's your top underwater speed now?'

'Nine and a half knots, sir.'

'What did I tell you! *My* first boat did ten! That was in the first world war!'

'We have advanced a little, sir, in many ways.'

'We've fitted *heads* in 'em now, if that's what you mean. When I joined my first boat as Pilot there were no heads. Used to get pretty constipated, I can tell you. The Captain and I, he's dead now poor fellow, used to sit out on either side of the tower in the mornings. One morning off the Scillies, I remember it well, we were sitting there, one on either side, when I heard a bloody great *thump* from the Captain's side. "Well *done*, sir!" I said. "Well done be buggered," he said, "that was my bloody binoculars!" '

The Reunion agenda had a reassuring permanence. A submariner returning after many years abroad would find the same people observing the same ritual as on his last visit. The programme was simple. It began with drinks, continued with a speech by the Senior Submariner, more drinks, a speech by the Admiral, more drinks, perhaps a speech by a visiting V.I.P. and ended with drinks.

The Senior Submariner made his speech as though he had left a lighted cigarette at the other end of the room and was anxious to get back to it. He welcomed everyone present to the Reunion, expressed his pleasure at seeing them there, hoped they would all enjoy themselves and stood down to a comfortable and thankful volume of applause.

'That's what I like about old Glueballs,' Dangerous Dan said to Wilfred irreverently. 'He always cuts it short.'

'There's something I've wanted to ask you for a long time, Dan. Does the Prime Minister really shoot over your land?'

'Of course not. We live in South Kensington. But I wasn't going to let that young snob get away with it. Good heavens, there's Black Sebastian! He looks more like Old Nick than ever. I wonder what he's doing here?'

Black Sebastian's presence at the Reunion had already caused a great deal of comment; his presence there was almost as incredible as the conversion of St Paul. He himself seemed to be aware of the incongruity and was wearing the artificial smile of a medieval torturer unaccountably forced to mix socially with his victims. He was talking to a man who had joined submarines at the same time but who had long ago left the Navy and taken up insurance.

'I can't think why we don't have far more Shop-Windows,' Black Sebastian was saying. 'Why tell a sailor to look out for submarines when nine times out of ten he hasn't the faintest idea what he's looking for?'

'Quite,' said the insurance man politely.

'Whenever a submarine does a Shop-Window for me I have it raising and lowering periscopes, radar masts, and snort mast until every sailor in my ship's company can tell me exactly which is which as soon as it breaks surface. It takes all day but I do it.'

'You always were an unreasonable sort of bastard, Sebastian,' said the insurance man, and walked away to get another drink.

Nearby, two very aged submariners were laughing into their whiskies.

'. . . Nobby, you've told me that story every year for forty years. I didn't think it funny forty years ago and I don't think it funny now. . . .'

Nobby stiffened.

'That's . . . that's exactly the sort of ill-mannered remark I expect from a man who never commanded anything better than a C-boat. . . .'

'I may tell you, the C-boats were the best submarines

God ever gave this earth. No C-boat captain would have had *you* anywhere near him. . . .'

After which unforgivable remark, the two very aged submariners moved sharply apart and cut each other dead for the rest of the Reunion, as they had done every year for the past forty.

The Lamm of God had been cornered by another aged submariner.

'. . . Then in 1923 I joined K.67 as Jimmy. God, what a boat! The captain, he died a good few years ago, was as queer as a nine-bob note. He used to read Omar Khayyam to the sailors every Sunday. He once shook Chief in the middle of the night because he'd just tried the whistle and thought it sounded A sharp instead of A flat. . . .'

The Admiral's Chief of Staff was hemmed in by yet another short-sighted and arthritic ancient.

'I'll give you some advice, boy. It was given to me by me first captain before the war, the first war that was, and I never forgot it. It was me first watch and I was as nervous as a virgin. I had the periscope goin' up and down like a whore's drawers. Then I heard water rushing somewhere in the control room bilges. When I told the Captain he said "Go and see what it is you stupid clot." Always run towards the sound of the water, he said. There you are. Always run towards the water at sea and the whisky in harbour. You're just starting out in life so I pass it on to you. So don't you forget that, heh?'

'Actually, I'm thinking of retiring next year,' said the Chief of Staff mildly.

'Heh?'

The Bodger was talking to a man who had the dark, ruddy tan of one who habitually worked out of doors. The Bodger was having a busy Reunion. It was some years since he had attended and he had many friends

197

there who came up to shake hands and demand the full story of the Targa Mango. The Reunion also gave The Bodger some moments of nostalgia; it seemed a long time since his first Reunion, when he and Commander S/M had removed the Admiral's trousers.

'It seems a long time since the first time, Paddy, doesn't it?' The Bodger said.

'Like last century.'

Paddy was wearing a shabby Cheviot tweed and black boots. He twisted his neck from side to side occasionally as though it was not often he wore a collar. He had long dark sideburns, a broad fleshy nose, and looked like a poacher. He had been a member of The Bodger's term at Dartmouth and now farmed a hundred acres in Shropshire.

'How's the farm going now?'

Paddy shrugged. 'So so. You can never tell with a farm. It takes about twenty years before you can really say. That's if you don't go bust in the first five. One thing *is* certain, I work a damn sight harder now than I ever did in the Service. Do my eyes deceive me, or is that Black Sebastian over there?'

'Yes. I was wondering what he was doing here myself.'

'*I* wonder how he ever lived as long as this. If ever there was a candidate for a quick shove over the side on a dark night, it's him. But tell me, Bodger, what's your future now?'

'I don't know. I was all set on retiring but all of a sudden this job in *Seahorse* dropped out of the blue. . . .'

'I heard about that. What actually *did* happen in that motor race. . . .'

Black Sebastian was talking to the Admiral.

'. . . I noticed when I was in the Med during the war that submarine losses followed a clear pattern. It was like a ski-ing holiday. You either break your leg on the first day or the last day. When a boat first came out, the first couple of patrols were the anxious ones. They were either so cautious they got thumped without ever knowing what happened or the Captain had been seeing too many Errol Flynn films and got thumped thinking he was God's gift to the war effort. Then they seemed to get into their stride and all was well. After about a year, the losses went up again. The Captain was over-confident or just plain worn out. I can see the same sort of thing happening again. . . .'

'Sir?'

The Chief of Staff appeared at the Admiral's elbow. The Admiral started, as though from a deep trance.

'Oh yes . . . My speech . . . Excuse me. . . .'

The Admiral Submarines' speech was the crux of the Reunion. The Admiral himself once described it as 'a mixture of a prize-giving speech, a chairman's annual report, and What The Stars Foretell.'

'Sssh,' said Dagwood to the group round him, 'the Speech from the Throne.'

'Gentlemen,' said the Admiral, 'while I was preparing this speech the other day and turning over a few of the things I might say in my mind, I came across some notes left by a predecessor of mine who was Admiral here just after the First World War. What he said then is still true now. The same words still apply. . . .'

'Because we're still using the same submarines,' a sardonic voice muttered, from the back.

'. . . He said: "I am convinced that the submarine has a greater future than any other weapon. I prophesy that one day the submarine will occupy the place the battle-ship holds now." You may think those unbelievably intelligent sentiments for an Admiral. . . .' The Admiral paused for laughter. '. . . But they must have seemed the words of a lunatic thirty years ago. They were said at a time when the Navy was sinking towards its lowest ebb since the reign of Charles II, when there was a strong move in international circles to ban the submarine altogether, as being *unfair*. That particular Admiral's listeners must have thought the old boy was a little touched in the head. He was indeed retired very soon afterwards. But now, those words are coming true. They are no longer the mad pronouncements of a visionary. They are almost a cliché. I believe that the nuclear submarine, which can fire a missile while still submerged, is the supreme strategical weapon. The world has seen nothing like it. The Submarine Service has been handed the instrument of Armageddon. It's a sobering thought to me that the young men we're now training as submariners may one day be in charge of a weapon which might have been measured for St Michael the Archangel. . . .'

Captain S/M leaned over to the Chief of Staff. 'You've been letting the Admiral read the newspapers again,' he whispered accusingly.

The Chief of Staff blushed and looked guilty.

'The Submarine Service is now approaching a period of great change. It is assuming greater importance every year. You can tell that it is growing in importance because the *Gunnery* Branch are trying to get in on it. Only today I squashed a proposal from Whale Island that our nuclear submarines should each carry a resident gunnery officer! I'm only sorry that I shan't be here to see these changes carried out but I know that my successor feels much as I do. . . .'

The Admiral was a moving speaker. He was a dedicated man, but full of humour. He also had an Admiral's essential quality, of optimism in public. When he had finished, those of his listeners still serving squared their shoulders, confident of good times and more submarines building just around the corner. Those who had retired began to feel that perhaps they had been too hasty.

'With any luck that should be all the speeches,' said Paddy.

'No,' said Commander S/M. 'We've got the visiting V.I.P. to come. Although it doesn't look as though he's turned up yet.'

The visiting V.I.P. did not in fact arrive until the company had been drinking for another two hours and had long forgotten all about speeches.

The Parliamentary Secretary to the Ministry of Political Warfare was a political chameleon. Like the Vicar of Bray, he remained whichever government was at Westminster. He had sat for an agricultural constituency in the West of England for more than forty years and had so impressed successive Prime Ministers with his ability that he was even now, at sixty-eight, still spoken of as a coming man. He had been on the fringe of power for so long that he had acquired the mannerisms of power itself. He walked and talked like a cabinet minister. His long years as a politician had given him a touch of absent-mindedness and an ability to speak at any time on any subject. The Chief of Staff had intended to ask the Minister himself but at the last minute had settled for the Parliamentary Secretary because he lived locally.

The Parliamentary Secretary knew exactly what was required of him. Apologising for his lateness, which he briskly blamed on a late sitting in the House, he brushed through the introductions and edged steadily nearer the dais whence, he knew with the infallible intuition of a born politician, the speeches were made. He was ready to speak long before his audience were ready to listen to him and was actually speaking before half of them were aware that he had arrived.

'Gentlemen,' said the Parliamentary Secretary, reading from a sheet of paper, 'may I say that I think it a great honour to be asked to speak at your Reunion. . . .'

'Who's that funny little man?' asked Dangerous Dan, who was on his fourteenth whisky.

'Some friend of the Chief of Staff's,' said someone, unjustly.

'. . . It has always been a pet theory of mine that the Anglo-Saxon races make the finest tank crews of any. If I may roughly paraphrase a favourite saying of the Emperor Charles V, To God I speak Spanish, to women Italian, to men French, and to my tank—English!'

The submariners raised their heads from their glasses in astonishment. The Bodger caught the Chief of Staff's look of mortal agony and shouted 'Hear hear!' in a resonant voice. A few others echoed the sentiment in a bewildered chorus.

'Thank you,' said the Parliamentary Secretary, simply. 'After all, we *invented* the tank! We perfected it. And we made brilliant use of it, all the way from the poppy-fields of Flanders to the desert sands of El Alamein.'

While the Chief of Staff stood wearing the unmistakable look of a Staff Officer when things are going irretrievably, ludicrously, wrong, the Parliamentary Secretary went on to describe a few of the more important technical advances in armoured warfare in recent years, to outline the careers of several outstanding armoured corps commanders, and to express his gratitude once more at being asked to attend the Reunion. It was a carefully composed speech for which someone had plainly done a lot of checking of facts and back-ground and it left the Reunion as well-informed about tanks as any group of submariners had ever been. On reaching the end of his sheet of paper, the Parliamentary Secretary folded it away, stepped down from the dais, accepted a drink, and made general conversation with the Chief of Staff and several other officers.

Anxious not to embarrass their guest, the Chief of Staff racked his brains for tank anecdotes. He saw Captain S/M standing on the outskirts of the circle. 'Don't just stand there,' he hissed frantically. 'Don't you know any Shaggy Tank stories?'

Captain S/M was more than equal to the emergency.

'I well remember taking command of my first Centurion. . . .' he began.

The wardroom hall porter touched Commander S/M's sleeve.

'Signal just come, sir.'

Commander S/M read the signal, gave a great hoot of jubilation, and showed it to Captain S/M. The signal's contents began to pass rapidly among the crowd. The Bodger, on the other side of the room, was suddenly aware that he had become the centre of attention.

'Congratulations, Bodger!'

In a moment, The Bodger was surrounded by eager hands competing to clap him on the back. A dozen voices shouted their congratulations. The Bodger himself was quite bewildered.

'But I don't understand it,' he kept saying. 'I was passed over. I was passed over some time ago.'

'Well there it is, Bodger, in black and white!'

'Let me see that signal again.'

'There is is. From Lieutenant Commander to Commander. Robert Bollinger Badger, H.M.S. *Seahorse*.'

'Well fillip me with a three-man beetle! This calls for a

drink! This calls for several drinks! But I still don't understand it. . . .'

'Don't look so baffled, Bodger,' said Commander S/M. 'You had to be promoted. The Press are already clamouring for it. Your drive in that race was the best piece of world-wide publicity for the Navy in many a year. The Army and the R.A.F. are green with envy, I can tell you. They're already planning their counter-measures, too. I hear the pongos are going in for the America Cup next year and the crab-fats are training a team to climb Everest. . . .'

'I must admit I had my doubts about you in *Seahorse*, Badger,' said the Admiral. 'I had a lot of doubts, I confess it. But it wasn't only that infernal motor race. You've made a damned good start in that ship. You were worth it on that alone.'

'I can't think why you've waited all this time, Bodger,' said Dangerous Dan, who was now on his twenty-fourth whisky.

'I'm sorry we're not all here, sir,' said Wilfred. 'I'm afraid the Midshipman is on a dirty week-end in Oozemouth. But for the rest of us, I can sincerely say "Congratulations," sir.'

'Badger?' said the Parliamentary Secretary. 'That's a familiar name.'

The Bodger prepared to tell the story of the Targa Mango again.

'Oh yes, I remember. Somebody sent me a docket a year or two ago marked "New Blood in Submarines." Well of course *I* don't know anything about submarines. Never have. But I did my best. I got out a list of Lieutenant Commanders and yours was the first name on the list. So I recommended you. Obviously I knew what I was doing, eh? Now, I must go, Admiral. I have another engagement tonight. I have to speak at the Southern Command Royal Tank Corps Old Comrades Association dinner. So I'll wish you good night. Good-bye, and thank you. Best of luck, Badger!'

Beaming genially to right and left, the Parliamentary Secretary went out to his car and drove off, leaving the Admiral, Captain S/M and The Bodger staring after him.

The Bodger's promotion set the seal on the Reunion. The noise redoubled. The Bodger's health was drunk in a variety of liquids. The atmosphere became charged with the authentic crackle of a successful party.

At three o'clock in the morning, The Bodger suddenly said: 'What was that the Admiral said in his speech about his successor? Is he going?'

'Haven't you heard?' said Commander S/M wearily. 'It's all been changed. Black Sebastian was promoted Rear Admiral today. He's going to be the next Admiral here.'

The Bodger raised his glass. 'Ah well,' he said. 'It's a funny life.'

(Continued from front flap)

the triumph of *Seahorse's* company, as formidable on the motor track as in the ocean, in the famous International Targa Mango da SanGuana in South America is the most publicized naval victory since Trafalgar. In face of desperate competition from world champions the *Seahorse* team drives to victory with an antique Land Rover, an equally venerable Armstrong-Siddeley, the SanGuana Police Chief's official daffodil and cerise Cadillac, and the co-operation of the local peasantry. The Bodger has clearly earned his promotion.

'John Winton' is the pseudonym for a young Engineer Officer in submarines in the Royal Navy. DOWN THE HATCH does not carry the usual disclaimer that references to actual persons or incidents are purely coincidental. Perhaps they are not.

ST MARTIN'S PRESS
175 Fifth Avenue
New York 10, N. Y.

Lightning Source UK Ltd.
Milton Keynes UK
UKHW022322070223
416659UK00004B/66